The Lady Paramount

Henry Harland

Alpha Editions

This edition published in 2022

ISBN : 9789356575486

Design and Setting By
Alpha Editions
www.alphaedis.com
Email - info@alphaedis.com

I

On the twenty-second anniversary of Susanna's birth, old Commendatore Fregi, her guardian, whose charge, by the provisions of her father's will, on that day terminated, gave a festa in her honour at his villa in Vallanza. Cannon had been fired in the morning: two-and-twenty salvoes, if you please, though Susanna had protested that this was false heraldry, and that it advertised her, into the bargain, for an old maid. In the afternoon there had been a regatta. Seven tiny sailing-boats, monotypes,—the entire fleet, indeed, of the Reale Yacht Club d'Ilaria—had described a triangle in the bay, with Vallanza, Presa, and Veno as its points; and I need n't tell anyone who knows the island of Sampaolo that the Marchese Baldo del Ponte's *Mermaid*, English name and all, had come home easily the first. Then, in the evening, there was a dinner, followed by a ball, and fire-works in the garden.

Susanna was already staying at the summer palace on Isola Nobile, for already—though her birthday falls on the seventeenth of April—the warm weather had set in; and when the last guests had gone their way, the Commendatore escorted her and her duenna, the Baroness Casaterrena, down through the purple Italian night, musical with the rivalries of a hundred nightingales, to the sea-wall, where, at his private landing-stage, in the bat-haunted glare of two tall electric lamps, her launch was waiting. But as he offered Susanna his hand, to help her aboard, she stepped quickly to one side, and said, with a charming indicative inclination of the head, "The Baronessa."

The precedence, of course, was rightfully her own. How like her, and how handsome of her, thought the fond old man, thus to waive it in favour of her senior. So he transferred his attention to the Baroness. She was a heavy body, slow and circumspect in her motions; but at length she had safely found her place among the silk cushions in the stern, and the Commendatore, turning back, again held out his hand to his sometime ward. As he was in the act of doing so, however, his ears were startled by a sound of puffing and of churning which caused him abruptly to face about.

"Hi! Stop!" he cried excitedly, for the launch was several yards out in the bay; and one could hear the Baroness, equally excited, expostulating with the man at the machine:

"He! Ferma, ferma!"

"It's all right," said Susanna, in that rather deep voice of hers, tranquil and leisurely; "my orders."

And the launch, unperturbed, held its course towards the glow-worm lights of Isola Nobile.

The Commendatore stared. . . .

For a matter of five seconds, his brows knitted together, his mouth half open, the Commendatore stared, now at Susanna, now after the bobbing lanterns of the launch,—whilst, clear in the suspension, the choir of nightingales sobbed and shouted.

"*Your* orders?" he faltered at last. Many emotions were concentrated in the pronoun.

"Yes," said Susanna, with a naturalness that perhaps was studied. "The first act of my reign."

He had never known her to give an order before, without asking permission; and this, in any case, was such an incomprehensible order. How, for instance, was she to get back to the palace?

"But how on earth," he puzzled, "will you get back to——"

"Oh, I 'm not returning to Isola Nobile tonight," Susanna jauntily mentioned, her chin a little perked up in the air. Then, with the sweetest smile—through which there pierced, perhaps, just a faint glimmer of secret mischief?—"I 'm starting on my wander-year," she added, and waved her hand imperially towards the open sea.

It was a progression of surprises for the tall, thin old Commendatore. No sooner had Susanna thus bewilderingly spoken, than the rub and dip of oars became audible, rhythmically nearing; and a minute after, from the outer darkness, a row-boat, white and slender, manned by two rowers in smart nautical uniforms, shot forward into the light, and drew up alongside the quay.

"A boat from the *Fiorimondo*," he gasped, in stupefaction.

"Yes," said Susanna, pleasantly. "The *Fiorimondo* takes me as far as Venice. There I leave it for the train."

The Commendatore's faded old blue eyes flickered anxiously.

"I can't think I am dreaming," he remarked, with a kind of vague plaintiveness; "and of course you are not serious. My dear, I don't understand."

"Oh, I 'm as serious as mathematics," she assured him.

She gave her head a little pensive movement of affirmation, and lifted her eyes to his, bright with an expression of trustful candour. This was an expression she was somewhat apt to assume when her mood was a teasing one; and it generally had the effect of breaking down the Commendatore's gravity. "You are a witch," he would laugh, availing himself without shame of the way-worn reproach, "a wicked, irresistible little witch."

"The thing," she explained, "is as simple as good-day. I 'm starting on my travels—to see the world—Paris, which I have only seen once—London, which I have never seen—the seaports of Bohemia, the mountains of Thule, which I have often seen from a distance, in the mists on the horizon. The *Fiorimondo* takes me as far as Venice. That is one of the advantages of owning a steam-yacht. Otherwise, I should have to go by the Austrian-Lloyd packet; and that would n't be half so comfortable."

Her eyes, still raised to the Commendatore's, melted in a smile;—a smile seemingly all innocence, persuasiveness, tender appeal for approbation, but (I 'm afraid) with an undergleam that was like a mocking challenge.

He, perforce, smiled too, though with manifest reluctance; and at the same time he frowned.

"My dear, if it were possible, I should be angry with you. This is scarcely an appropriate hour for mystifications."

"*That* it is n't," agreed Susanna, heartily. And she put up her hand, to cover a weary little yawn. "But there 's *no* mystification. There 's a perfectly plain statement of fact. I 'm starting to-night for Venice."

He studied her intently for a moment, fixedly, pondering something. Then, all at once, the lines of dismay cleared from his lean old ivory-yellow face.

"Ha! In a ball-dress," he scoffed, and pointed a finger at Susanna's snowy confection of tulle and satin and silver embroidery, all a-shimmer in the artificial moonlight of the electric lamps, against the background of southern garden,—the outlines and masses, dim and mysterious in the night, of palms and cypresses, of slender eucalyptus-trees, oleanders, magnolias, of orange-trees, where the oranges hung, amid the dark foliage, like dull-burning lanterns. A crescent of diamonds twinkled in the warm blackness of her hair. She wore a collar of pearls round her throat, and a long rope of pearls that descended to her waist, and was then looped up and caught at the bosom by an opal clasp. A delicate perfume, like the perfume of violets, came and went in the air near her. She held a great fluffy fan of white feathers in one hand, and in the other carried loose her long white gloves; and gems sparkled on her fingers. The waters under the sea-wall beside her kept up a perpetual whispering, like a commentary on the situation. The old man considered these things, and his misgivings were entirely dissipated.

"Ha!" he scoffed, twisting his immense iron-grey moustaches with complacency. "I can't guess what prank you may be up to, but you are never starting for Venice in a ball-dress. You 're capable of a good deal, my dear, but you 're not capable of that."

"Oh, I 'm capable of anything and everything," Susanna answered, cheerfully ominous. "Besides," she plausibly admonished him, "you might do me the justice of supposing that I have changes aboard the *Fiorimondo*. My maid awaits me there with quite a dozen boxes. So—you see. Oh, and by the bye," she interjected, "Serafino also is coming with me. He'll act as courier—buy my tickets, register my luggage; and then, when we reach our ultimate destination, resume his white cap and apron. My ultimate destination, you must know," she said, with a lightness which, I think, on the face of it was spurious, "is a little village in England—a little village called Craford; and"—she smiled convincingly—"I hear that the cuisine is not to be depended upon in little English villages."

All the Commendatore's anxieties had revived. This time he frowned in grim earnest.

"*Créforrrà!*" he ejaculated.

The word fell like an explosion; and there was the climax of horrified astonishment in those reverberating r's.

"I think you are mad," he said. "Or, if you are not mad, you are the slyest young miss in Christendom."

Susanna's eyes darkened, pathetic, wistful.

"Ah, don't be cross," she pleaded. "I 'm not mad, and I 'm not sly. But I 'm free and independent. What's the good of being free and independent," she largely argued, "if you can't do the things you want to? I 'm going to Craford to realise the aspiration of a lifetime. I 'm going to find out my cousin, and make his acquaintance, and see what he 's like. And then—well, if he 's nice, who knows what may happen? I planned it ever so long ago," she proclaimed, with an ingenuousness that was almost brazen, "and made all my preparations. Then I sat down and waited for the day when I should be free and independent."

Her eyes melted again, deprecating his censure, beseeching his indulgence, yet still, with a little glint of raillery, defying him to do his worst.

His hand sawed the air, his foot tapped the ground.

"Free and independent, free and independent," he fumed, in derision. "Fine words, fine words. And you made all your preparations beforehand, in secrecy; and you 're not sly? Misericordia di Dio!"

He groaned impotently; he shook his bony old fist at the stars in the firmament.

"Perhaps you will admit," he questioned loftily, "that there are decencies to be observed even by the free and independent? It is not decent for you to travel alone. If you mean a single word of what you say, why are n't you accompanied by the Baronessa?"

"The Baronessa fatigues me," Susanna answered gently. "And I exasperate her and try her patience cruelly. She 's always putting spokes in my wheel, and I 'm always saying and doing things she disapproves of. Ah, if she only suspected the half of the things I don't say or do, but think and feel!"

She nodded with profound significance.

"We belong," she pointed out, "to discrepant generations. I 'm so intensely modern, and she 's so irredeemably eighteen-sixty. I 've only waited for this blessed day of liberty to cut adrift from the Baronessa. And the pleasure will be mutual, I promise you. She will enjoy a peace and a calm that she has n't known for ages. Ouf! I feel like Europe after the downfall of Napoleon."

She gave her shoulders a little shake of satisfaction.

"The Baronessa," she said, and I 'm afraid there was laughter in her tone, "is a prisoner for the night on Isola Nobile." I 'm afraid she tittered. "I gave orders that the launch was to start off the moment she put her foot aboard it, and on no account was it to turn back, and on no account was any boat to leave the island till to-morrow morning. I expect she 'll be rather annoyed—and puzzled. But—cosa vuole? It's all in the day's work."

Then her voice modulated, and became confidential and exultant.

"I 'm going to have such a delicious plunge. See—to-night I have put on pearls, and diamonds, and rings, that the Baronessa would never let me wear. And I 've got a whole bagful of books, to read in the train—Anatole France, and Shakespeare, and Gyp, and Pierre Loti, and Molière, and Max Beerbohm, and everybody: all the books the Baronessa would have died a thousand deaths rather than let me look at. That's the nuisance of being a woman of position—you 're brought up never to read anything except the Lives of the Saints and the fashion papers. I 've had to do all my really important reading by stealth, like a thief in the night. Ah," she sighed, "if I were only a man, like you! But as for observing the decencies," she continued briskly, "you need have no fear. I 'm going to the land of all lands where (if report speaks true) one has most opportunities of observing them—I 'm going to England, and I 'll observe them with both eyes. And I 'm not travelling alone." She spurned the imputation. "There are Rosina and Serafino; and at the end of my journey I shall have Miss Sandus. You remember that nice Miss Sandus?" she asked, smiling up at him. "She is my fellow-conspirator. We arranged it all before she went away last autumn. I 'm to go to her house in London, and she will go with me to Craford. She 's frantically interested about my cousin. She thinks it's the most thrilling and romantic story she has ever heard. And she thoroughly sympathises with my desire to make friends with him, and to offer him some sort of reparation."

The Commendatore was pacing nervously backwards and forwards, being, I suppose, too punctilious an old-school Latin stickler for etiquette to interrupt.

But now, "Curse her for a meddlesome Englishwoman," he spluttered violently. "To encourage a young girl like you in such midsummer folly. A young girl?—a young hoyden, a young tom-boy. What? You will travel from here to London without a chaperon? And books—French novels—gr-r-r! I wish you had never been taught to read. I think it is ridiculous to teach women to read. What good will they get by reading? You deserve—upon my word you deserve . . . Well, never mind. Oh, body of Bacchus!"

He wrung his hands, as one in desperation.

"A young girl, a mere child," he cried, in a wail to Heaven; "a mere"—he paused, groping for an adequate definition—"a mere irresponsible female orphan! And nobody with power to interfere."

Susanna drew herself up.

"Young?" she exclaimed. "A mere child? I? Good gracious, I 'm *twenty-two*."

She said it, scanning the syllables to give them weight, and in all good faith I think, as who should say, "I 'm fifty."

"You really can't accuse me of being young," she apodictically pronounced. "I 'm twenty-two. Twenty-two long years—aïe, Dio mio! And I look even older. I could pass for twenty-five. If," was her suddenly-inspired concession, "if it will afford you the least atom of consolation, I 'll *tell* people that I am twenty-five. *There*."

She wooed him anew with those melting eyes, and her tone was soft as a caress.

"It is n't every man that I 'd offer to sacrifice three of the best years of my life for—and it is n't every man that I 'd offer to tell fibs for."

She threw back her head, and stood in an attitude to invite inspection.

"Don't I look twenty-five?" she asked. "If you had n't the honour of my personal acquaintance, would it ever occur to you that I 'm what you call 'a young girl'? Would n't you go about enquiring of every one, 'Who is that handsome, accomplished, and perfectly dressed woman of the world?'"

And she made him the drollest of little quizzical moues.

In effect, with her tall and rather sumptuously developed figure, with the humour and vivacity, the character and decision, of her face, with the glow deep in her eyes, the graver glow beneath the mirth that danced near their surface,—and then too, perhaps, with the unequivocal Southern richness of her colouring: the warm white and covert rose of her skin, the dense black of her undulating abundant hair, the sudden, sanguine red of her lips,—I think you would have taken her for more than twenty-two. There was nothing of the immature or the unfinished, nothing of the tentative, in her aspect. With no loss of freshness, there were the strength, the poise, the assurance, that we are wont to associate with a riper womanhood. Whether she looked twenty-five or not, she looked, at any rate, a completed product; she looked distinguished and worth while; she looked alive, alert: one in whom the blood coursed swiftly, the spirit burned vigorously; one who would love her pleasure, who could be wayward and provoking, but who could also be generous and loyal; she looked high-bred, one in whom there was race, as well as temperament and nerve.

The Commendatore, however, was a thousand miles from these considerations. He glared fiercely at her—as fiercely as it was *in* his mild old eyes to glare. He held himself erect and aloof, in a posture that was eloquent of haughty indignation.

"I will ask your Excellency a single question. Are you or are you not the Countess of Sampaolo?" he demanded sternly.

But Susanna was incorrigible.

"At your service—unless I was changed at nurse," she assented, dropping a curtsey; and an imp laughed in her eyes.

"And are you aware," the Commendatore pursued, with the tremor of restrained passion in his voice, "that the Countess of Sampaolo, a countess in her own right, is a public personage? Are you aware that the actions you are proposing—which would be disgraceful enough if you were any little obscure bourgeoise—must precipitate a public scandal? Have you reflected that it will all be printed in the newspapers, for men to snigger at in their cafes, for women to cackle over in their boudoirs? Have you reflected that you will make yourself a nine-days' wonder, a subject for tittle-tattle with all the gossip-mongers of Europe? Are you without pride, without modesty?"

Susanna arched her eyebrows, in amiable surprise.

"Oh?" she said. "Have I omitted to mention that I 'm to do the whole thing in masquerade? How stupid of me. Yes,"—her voice became explanatory,—"it's essential, you see, that my cousin Antonio should never dream who I really am. He must fancy that I 'm just anybody—till the time comes for me to cast my domino, and reveal the fairy-princess. So I travel under a nom-de-guerre. I 'm a widow, a rich, charming, dashing, not too-disconsolate widow; and my name . . . is Madame Fregi."

She brought out the last words after an instant's irresolution, and marked them by a hazardous little smile.

"What!" thundered the Commendatore. "You would dare to take *my* name as a cloak for your escapades? I forbid it. Understand. I peremptorily forbid it."

He stamped his foot, he nodded his outraged head, menacingly.

But Susanna was indeed incorrigible.

"Dear me," she grieved; "I hoped you would be touched by the compliment. How strange men are. Never mind, though," she said, with gay resignation. "I 'll call myself something else. Let's think. . . . Would—would Torrebianca do?" Her eyes sought counsel from his face.

Torrebianca, I need n't remind those who are familiar with Sampaolo, is the name of a mountain, a bare, white, tower-like peak of rock, that rises in the middle of the island, the apex of the ridge separating the coast of Vallanza from the coast of Orca.

"Madame Torrebianca? La Nobil Donna Susanna Torrebianca?" She tried the name on her tongue. "Yes, for an impromptu, Torrebianca is n't bad. It's picturesque, and high-sounding, and yet not—not *invraisemblable*. You don't think it *invraisemblable*? So here 's luck to that bold adventuress, that knightess-errant, the widow Torrebianca."

She raised her fluffy white fan, as if it were a goblet from which to quaff the toast, and flourished it aloft.

The poor old Commendatore was mumbling helpless imprecations in his moustache. One caught the word "atrocious" several times repeated.

"And now," said Susanna brightly, "kiss me on both cheeks, and give me your benediction."

She moved towards him, and held up her face.

But he drew away.

"My child," he began, impressively, "I have no means to constrain you, and I know by experience that when you have made up that perverse little mind of yours, one might as well attempt to reason with a Hebrew Jew. Therefore I can only beg, I can only implore. I implore you not to do this fantastic, this incredible, this unheard-of thing. I will go on my knees to you. I will entreat you, not for my sake, but for your own sake, for the sake of your dead father and mother, to put this ruinous vagary from you, to abandon this preposterous journey, and to stay quietly here in Sampaolo. Then, if you must open up the past, if you must get into communication with your distant cousin, I 'll help you to find some other, some sane and decorous method of doing so."

Still once again Susanna's eyes melted, but there was no mockery in them now.

"You are kind and patient," she said, with feeling; "and I hate to be a brute. Yet what is there to do? I can't alter my resolution. And I can't bear to refuse you when you talk to me like that. So—you must forgive me if I take a brusque way of escaping the dilemma."

She ran to the edge of the quay, and sprang lightly into her boat.

"Avanti—avanti," she cried to the rowers, who instantly pushed the boat free, and bent upon their oars.

Then she waved her disfranchised guardian a kiss.

"Addio, Commendatore. I 'll write to you from Venice."

II

It was gay June weather, in a deep green English park: a park in the south of England, near the sea, where parks are deepest and greenest, and June weather, when it is n't grave, is gaiest. Blackbirds were dropping their liquid notes, thrushes were singing, hidden in the trees. Here and there, in spaces enclosed by hurdles, sheep browsed or drowsed, still faintly a-blush from recent shearing. The may was in bloom, the tardy may, and the laburnum. The sun shone ardently, and the air was quick with the fragrant responses of the earth.

A hundred yards up the avenue, Anthony Craford stopped his fly, a shabby victoria, piled with the manifold leather belongings of a traveller, and dismounted.

"I 'll walk the rest of the way," he said to the flyman, giving him his fare. "Drive on to the house. The servants will take charge of the luggage."

"Yes, sir," answered the flyman, briskly, and flicked his horse: whereat, displaying a mettle one was by no means prepared for, the horse dashed suddenly off in a great clattering gallop, and the ancient vehicle behind him followed with a succession of alarming leaps and lurches.

"See," declaimed a voice, in a sort of whimsical recitative,

"See how the young cabs bound,
As to the tabor's sound,—"

a full-bodied baritone, warm and suave, that broke, at the end, into a note or two of laughter.

Anthony turned.

On the greensward, a few paces distant, stood a man in white flannels: rather a fat man, to avow the worst at once, but, for the rest, distinctly a pleasant-looking; with a smiling, round, pink face, smooth-shaven, and a noticeable pair of big and bright blue eyes.

"Hello. Is that you, old Rosygills?" Anthony said, with a phlegm that seemed rather premeditated.

"Now, what a question," protested the other, advancing to meet him. He walked with an odd kind of buoyant, measured step, as if he were keeping time to a silent dance-tune. "All I can tell you is that it's someone very nice and uncommonly like me. You should know at your age that a person's identity is quite the most mysterious mystery under heaven. You really must n't expect me to vouch for mine. How-d'ye-do?"

He extended, casually, in the manner of a man preoccupied, a plump, pink left hand. With his right hand he held up and flaunted, for exhibition, a drooping bunch of poppies, poignantly red and green: the subject, very likely, of his preoccupation, for, "Are n't they beauties?" he demanded, and his manner had changed to one of fervour, nothing less. "They 're the spoils of a raid on Farmer Blogrim's chalk-pit. If eyes were made for seeing, see and admire—admire and confess your admiration."

He shook them at Anthony's face. But as Anthony looked at them with composure, and only muttered, "H'm," "Oh, my little scarlet starlets," he purred and chirped to the blossoms, "*would n't* the apathetic man admire you?"

And he clasped them to his bosom with a gesture that was reminiscent of the grateful prima-donna.

"They look exactly as if I had plucked them from the foreground of a Fifteenth Century painting, don't they?" he went on, holding them off again. "Florentine, of course. Ah, in those days painting was a fine art, and worth a rational being's consideration,—in those days, and in just that little Tuscan corner of the world. But you," he pronounced in deep tones, mournfully, "how cold, how callous, you are. Have you no soul for the loveliness of flowers?"

Anthony sighed. He was a tall young man, (thirty, at a guess), tall and well set-up, with grey eyes, a wholesome brown skin, and a nose so affirmatively patrician in its high bridge and slender aquilinity that it was a fair matter for remark to discover it on the face of one who actually chanced to be of the patrician order. Such a nose, perhaps, carried with it certain obligations—an obligation of fastidious dressing, for example. Anthony, at any rate, was very fastidiously dressed indeed, in light-grey tweeds, with a straw hat, and a tie that bespoke a practised hand beside a discerning taste. But his general air, none the less,—the expression of his figure and his motions, as well as of his face and voice,—was somehow that of an indolent melancholy, a kind of unresentful disenchantment, as if he had long ago perceived that cakes are mostly dough, and had accommodated himself to the perception with a regret that was half amusement.

His friend, by contrast, in loose white flannels, with a flannel shirt and a leather belt, with yellowish hair, waving, under a white flannel cricket-cap, a good inch longer than the conventional cut, was plainly a man who set himself above the modes: though, in his plump, pink way debonair and vivacious, not so tall as Anthony, yet tall enough never to be contemned as short, and verging upon what he was fain to call "the flower of a sound man's youth, the golden, gladsome, romantic age of forty," he looked delightfully fresh, and wide-awake, and cheerful, and perfectly in the scheme of the blue day and the bird-notes and the smiling country. Permit me to introduce Mr. Adrian Willes, by vocation a composer and singer of songs, and—"contrapuntally," as he would explain—Anthony Craford's housemate, monitor, land-agent, and man of business.

Anthony sighed.

"I 'll tell you what I admire," he answered drily. "I admire the transports of delight with which you hail my unexpected home-coming. The last you knew, I was in California; and here I might have tumbled from the skies."

Adrian regarded him with an eye in which, I think, kindled a certain malicious satisfaction.

"Silence," he said, "is the perfectest herald of joy. Besides, you must n't flatter yourself that your home-coming is so deucedly unexpected, either. I 've felt a pricking in my thumbs any time these three months; and no longer ago than yesterday morning, I said to my image in the glass, as I was shaving, 'I should n't wonder if Tony turned up to-morrow,' said I."

"That was merely your uneasy conscience," Tony expounded. "When the cat's away, the mice are always feeling prickings in their thumbs."

"Oh, if you stoop to bandying proverbs," retaliated Adrian, "there's a proverb about a penny." He raised his bunch of poppies, and posed it aloft before him, eyeing it, his head cocked a little to one side, in critical enjoyment. "Shall we set out for the house?" he asked.

"No," said Anthony, promptly, with decision. "*I 'll* set out for the house; and *you* (unless your habits have strangely altered) will frisk and gambol round about me. Come on."

And taking Adrian's arm, he led the way, amid the summer throng of delicate scents and sounds, under the opulent old trees, over the gold-green velvet of the turf, on which leaves and branches were stencilled by the sun, as in an elaborate design for lace, towards a house that was rather famous in the neighbourhood—I was on the point of saying for its beauty: but are things ever famous in English neighbourhoods for their mere beauty?—for its quaintness, and in some measure too, perhaps, for its history:—Craford Old Manor, a red-brick Tudor house, low, and, in the rectangular style of such houses, rambling; with a paved inner court, and countless tall chimneys, like minarets; with a secret chapel and a priests' "hiding-hole," for the Crafords were one of those old Catholic families whose boast it is that they "have never lost the Faith"; with a walled formal garden, and a terrace, and a sun-dial; with close-cropped bordures of box, and yews clipped to fantastic patterns: the house so placed withal, that, while its north front faced the park, its south front, ivy-covered, looked over a bright lawn and bright parterres of flowers, down upon the long green levels of Rowland Marshes, and away to the blue sea beyond,—the blue sea, the white cliffs, the yellow sands.

Anthony and Adrian, arm in arm, sauntered on without speaking, till they attained the crest of a sweeping bit of upland, and the house and the sea came in view. Here they halted, and stood for a minute in contemplation of the prospect.

"The sea," said Adrian, disengaging his arm, that he might be free to use it as a pointer, and then pointing with it, "the sea has put on her bluest frock, to honour your return. And behold, decked in the hues of Iris, that gallant procession of cliffs, like an army with banners, zigzagging up from the world's rim, to bid you welcome. Oh, you were clearly not unexpected. If no smoke rises from yonder chimneys,—if your ancestral chimney-stone is cold,—that's merely because, despite the season, we 're having a spell of warmish weather, and we 've let the fires go out. 'T is June. Town 's full; country 's depopulated. In Piccadilly, I gather from the public prints, vehicular traffic is painfully congested. Meanwhile, I 've a grand piece of news for your private ear. Guess a wee bit what it is."

"Oh, I 'm no good at guessing," said Anthony, with languor, as they resumed their walk.

"Well—what will you give me, then, if I 'll blurt it out?" asked Adrian, shuffling along sidewise, so that he might face his companion.

"My undivided attention—provided you blurt it briefly," Anthony promised.

"Oh, come," Adrian urged, swaying his head and shoulders. "Betray a little curiosity, at least."

"Curiosity is a vice I was taught in my youth to suppress," said Anthony.

"A murrain on your youth," cried Adrian, testily. "However, since there 's no quieting you otherwise, I suppose, for the sake of peace, I 'd best tell you, and have done with it. Well, then,"—he stood off, to watch the effect of his announcement,—"Craford's Folly is let."

"Ah?" said Anthony, with no sign of emotion.

Adrian's face fell.

"Was there ever such inhumanity?" he mourned. "I tell him that—thanks to my supernatural diligence in his affairs—his own particular millstone is lifted from his neck. I tell him that a great white elephant of a house, which for years has been eating its head off, and keeping him poor, is at last—by my supernatural diligence—converted into an actual source of revenue. And 'Ah?' is all he says, as if it did n't concern him. Blow, blow, thou winter wind,—thou art not so unkind as Man's ingratitude."

"Silence," Anthony mentioned, "is the perfectest herald of joy."

"Pish, tush," said Adrian. "A fico for the phrase. I 'll bet a shilling, all the same,"—and he scanned Anthony's countenance apprehensively,—"that you 'll be wanting money?"

"It's considered rather low," Anthony generalised, "to offer a bet on what you have every ground for regarding as a certainty."

"A certainty?" groaned Adrian. He tossed his plump arms heavenwards. "There it is! He 's wanting money."

And his voice broke, in something like a sob.

"Do you know," he asked, "how many pounds sterling you 've had the spending of during the past twelvemonth? Do you know how many times your poor long-suffering bankers have written to me, with tears in their eyes, to complain that your account was overdrawn, and would I be such a dear as to set it right? No? You don't? I could have sworn you did n't. Well, I do—to my consternation. And it is my duty to caution you that the estate won't stand it—to call that an estate," he divagated, with a kind of despairing sniff, "which is already, by the extravagances of your ancestors, shrunken to scarcely more than three acres and a cow. You 're wanting money? What do you *do* with your money? What secret profligacy must a man be guilty of, who squanders such stacks of money? Burst me, if I might n't as well be steward to a bottomless pit. However, Providence be praised,—and my own supernatural diligence,—I 'm in command of quite unhoped-for resources. Craford New Manor is let."

"So you remarked before," said Anthony, all but yawning.

"And shall again, if the impulse seizes me," Adrian tartly rejoined. "The circumstance is a relevant and a lucky one for the man you 're fondest of, since he's wanting money. If it were n't that the new house is let, he 'd find my pockets in the condition of Lord Tumtoddy's noddle. However, the saints are merciful, I 'm a highly efficient agent, and the biggest, ugliest, costliest house in all this countryside is let."

"Have it so, dear Goldilocks," said Anthony, with submission. "I 'll ne'er deny it more."

"There would be no indiscretion," Adrian threw out, "in your asking whom it's let to."

"Needless to ask," Anthony threw back. "It's let to a duffer, of course. None but a duffer would be duffer enough to take it."

"Well, then, you 're quite mistaken," said Adrian, airily swaggering. "It's let to a lady."

"Oh, there be lady duffers," Anthony apprised him.

"It's very ungallant of you to say so." Adrian frowned disapprobation. "This lady, if you can bear to hear the whole improbable truth at once, is an Italian lady."

"An Italian lady? Oh?" Anthony's interest appeared to wake a little.

Adrian laughed.

"I expected that would rouse you. A Madame Torrebianca."

"Ah?" said Anthony; and his interest appeared to drop.

"Yes—la Nobil Donna Susanna Torrebianca. Is n't that a romantic name? A lady like the heroine of some splendid old Italian story,—like Pompilia, like Francesca,—like Kate the Queen, when her maiden was binding her tresses. Young, and dark, and beautiful, and altogether charming."

"H'm. And not a duffer? An adventuress, then, clearly," said Anthony. "You 'll never get the rent."

"Nothing of the sort," Adrian asserted, with emphasis. "A lady of the highest possible respectability. Trust me to know. A scrupulous Catholic, besides. It was partly because we have a chapel that she decided to take the house. Father David is hand and glove with her. And rich. She gave the very best of banker's references. 'Get the rent,' says he—as if I had n't got my quarter in advance. I let furnished—what? Well, that's the custom—rent payable quarterly in advance. And cultivated. She's read everything, and she prattles English like you or me. She had English governesses when she was a kiddie. And appreciative. She thinks I 'm without exception the nicest man she 's ever met. She adores my singing, and delights in all the brilliant things I say. She says things that are n't half bad herself, and plays my accompaniments with really a great deal of sympathy and insight. And Tony dear,"—he laid his hand impressively on Tony's arm, while his voice sank to the pitch of deep emotion,—"she has a cook—a cook—ah, me!"

He smacked his lips, as at an unutterable recollection.

"She brought him with her from Italy. He has a method of preparing sweetbreads—well, you wait. His name is Serafino—and no wonder. And she has the nicest person who was ever born to live with her: a Miss Sandus, Miss Ruth Sandus, a daughter of the late Admiral Sir Geoffrey Sandus. She 's a dove, she 's a duck, she 's a darling; she 's completely won my heart. And I"—he took a few skipping steps, and broke suddenly into song—

"'And I, and I have hers!'

We dote upon each other. She calls me her Troubadour. She has the prettiest hands of any woman out of Paradise. She 's as sweet as remembered kisses after death. She 's as sharp as a needle. She 's as bright as morning roses lightly tipped with dew. She has a house of her own in Kensington. And she's seventy-four years of age."

Anthony's interest appeared to wake again.

"Seventy-four? You call that young?" he asked, with the inflection of one who was open to be convinced.

Adrian bridled.

"You deliberately put a false construction on my words. I was alluding to Miss Sandus, as you 're perfectly well aware. Madame Torrebianca is n't seventy-four, nor anything near it. She's not twenty-four. Say about twenty-five and a fraction. With such hair too—and such frocks—and eyes. Oh, my dear!" He kissed his fingers, and wafted the kiss to the sky. "Eyes! Imagine twin moons rising over a tropical—"

"*Allons donc*," Anthony repressed him. "Contain yourself. Where is Madame Torrebianca's husband?"

"Ah," said Adrian, with a sudden lapse of tone. "Where is Madame Torrebianca's husband? That's the question. Where?" And he winked suggestively. "How can I tell you where he is? If I could tell you that, you don't suppose I 'd be wearing myself to a shadow with uncongenial and ill-remunerated labour, in an obscure backwater of the country, like this, do you? If I could tell you that, I could tell you the secretest secrets of the sages, and I should be making my everlasting fortune—oh, but money hand over fist—as the oracle of a general information bureau, in Bond Street, or somewhere. I should be a millionaire, and a celebrity, and a regular cock-of-the-walk. Where is Madame Torrebianca's husband? Ay! Gentle shepherd, tell me where?"

"Ah?" wondered Anthony, off his guard. "A mysterious disappearance?"

"Bravo!" crowed Adrian, gleefully. "I am not only witty myself, but the cause of wit in others." He patted Anthony on the shoulder. "A mysterious disappearance. The *mot* is capital. That's it, to a hair's breadth. Oft thought before, but ne'er so well expressed. The gentleman (as the rude multitude in their unfeeling way would put it) is dead."

"On the whole," mused Anthony, looking him up and down with a reflective eye, "you 're an effulgent sort of egotist, as egotists go; but you yield much cry for precious little wool."

"Yes, dead," Adrian repeated, pursuing his own train of ideas. "Donna Susanna is a widow, a poor lone widow, a wealthy, eligible widow. You must be kind to her."

"Why don't you marry her?" Anthony enquired.

"Pooh," said Adrian.

"Why don't you?" Anthony insisted. "If she 's really rich? You don't dislike her—you respect her—perhaps, if you set your mind to it, you could even learn to love her. She 'd give you a home and a position in the world; she 'd make a sober citizen of you; and she 'd take you off my hands. You know whether you 're an expense—and a responsibility. Why don't you marry her? You owe it to me not to let such an occasion slip."

"Pooh," said Adrian. But he looked conscious, and he laughed a deliriously conscious laugh. "What nonsense you do talk. I 'm too young, I 'm far too young, to think of marrying."

"See him blush and giggle and shake his pretty curls," said Anthony, with scorn, addressing the universe.

By this time they had skirted the house, and come round to the southern front, where the sunshine lay unbroken on the lawn, and the smell of the box hedges, strong in the still air, seemed a thing almost ponderable: the low, long front, a mellow line of colour, with the purple of its old red bricks and the dark green of its ivy, sunlit against the darker green of the park, and the blue of the tender English sky. The terrace steps were warm under their feet, as they mounted them. In terra-cotta urns, at intervals upon the terrace balustrade, roses grew, roses red and white; and from larger urns, one at either side of the hall-door, red and white roses were espaliered, intertwining overhead.

The hall-door stood open; but the hall, as they entered it from the brightness without, was black at first, like a room unlighted. Then, little by little, it turned from black to brown, and defined itself:—"that hackneyed type of Stage-property hall," I have heard Adrian lament, "which connotes immediately a lost will, a family secret, and the ghost of a man in armour";

"a noble apartment, square and spacious, characteristic of the period when halls were meant to serve at need as guard-rooms," says the *County History*.

Square and spacious it was certainly, perhaps a hackneyed type none the less: the ceiling and the walls panelled in dark well-polished oak; the floor a pavement of broad stone flags, covered for the most part now by a faded Turkey carpet; the narrow windows, small-paned and leaded, set in deep stone embrasures; a vast fireplace jutting across a corner, the Craford arms emblazoned in the chimney-piece above; and a wide oak staircase leading to the upper storey. The room was furnished, incongruously enough, in quite a modern fashion, rather shabbily, and I daresay rather mannishly. There were leather arm-chairs and settles, all a good deal worn, and stout tables littered with books and periodicals. The narrow windows let in thin slants of mote-filled sunshine, vortices of gold-dust; and on the faded carpet, by the door, lay a bright parallelogram, warming to life its dim old colours. The rest of the room seemed twilit. Someone had been too wise to defeat that good oak panelling by hanging pictures on it.

"Not a creature is stirring," said Adrian, "not even a mouse. Sellers—oh, what men daily do, not knowing what they do!—is shut up in the scullery, I suppose, torturing his poor defenceless fiddle. That 's what it is to be a musical boot-and-knife boy. And Wickersmith will be at his devotions. He tells me he never gets leisure for his morning meditation till luncheon 's cleared away. And that's what it is to be a pious butler. I 'm doubting whether there was anyone to disembarrass that flyman of yours of your luggage. So he 's probably driven off with it all to his humble, happy home. I see none of it about. Never mind. There 'll be some of your old things in Mrs. W.'s camphor-chest, perhaps; or if it comes to a pinch, I can lend you a garment or so of my own,—and then won't Craford of Craford cut a figure of fun! You will make her acquaintance . . . Let me see. To-day is Wednesday. We 'll call on her to-morrow."

"On whom?" asked Anthony, looking blank.

"Have we been talking of Queen Berengaria?" Adrian, with his nose in the air, enquired. "On *whom?* says you. We 'll call to-morrow afternoon."

"Not I," said Anthony.

"Not to-morrow?" Adrian raised his eyebrows, well-marked crescents of reddish-brown above his ruddy face, and assumed thereby a physiognomy of almost childlike naïveté. "Ah, well, on Friday, then;—though Friday is unlucky, and one rarely shines on a day of abstinence, anyhow. It's all a fallacy about fish being food for the brain. Meat, red meat, is what the brain requires." He slapped his forehead. "But Friday, since you prefer it."

Anthony seated himself on the arm of a leather chair, and, with calculated deliberation, produced his cigarette-case, selected a cigarette, returned his cigarette-case to his pocket, took out his matchbox, struck a match, and got his cigarette alight.

"No, dear Nimbletongue," he said at last, through a screen of smoke, "not Friday, either." He smiled, shaking his head.

Disquiet began to paint itself in Adrian's mien.

"Name your own day." He waited, anxious, in suspense.

Anthony chuckled.

"My own day is no day. I have n't the faintest desire to make the good woman's acquaintance, and I shall not call on her at all."

Adrian stretched out appealing hands.

"But Anthony—" he adjured him.

"No," said Anthony, with determination. "I 'm not a calling man. And I 've come down here for rest and recreation. I 'll pay no calls. Let that be understood. Calls, quotha! And in the country, at that. Oh, don't I know them? Oh, consecrated British dulness! The smug faces, the vacuous grins; the lifeless, limping attempts at conversation; the stares of suspicious incomprehension if you chance to say a thing that has a point; and then, the thick, sensible, slightly muddy boots. I 'll pay no calls. And as for making acquaintances—save me from those I 've made already. In broad England I can recall but three acquaintances who are n't of a killing sameness;—and one of those," he concluded sadly, with a bow to his companion, "one of those is fat, and grows old."

"Poor lad," Adrian commiserated him. "You are tired and overwrought. Go to your room, and have a bath and a brush up. That will refresh you. Then, at half-past four, you can renew the advantages of my society at tea in the garden. Oh, you 'll find your room quite ready. I 've felt a pricking in my thumbs any time these three months. Shall I send Wick?"

"Yes, if you will be so good," said Anthony. He rose, and moved towards the staircase.

Adrian waited till he had reached the top.

Then, "You 'll meet her whether you like or not on Sunday. Where on earth do you suppose she hears her Mass?" he called after him.

"Oh, hang," Anthony called back.

For, sure enough, unless she drove seven miles to Wetherleigh, where could she hear her Mass, but as his guest, in the chapel of his house?

III

Susanna was seated on the moss, at the roots of a wide-spreading oak. She was leaning back, so that she could look up, up, through vistas of changing greens,—black-green to gold-green,—through a thousand labyrinthine avenues and counter-avenues of leaves and branches, with broken shafts of sunlight caught in them here and there, to the glimpses of blue sky visible beyond. The tree gave you a sense of great spaces, and depths, and differences, like a world; and it was full of life, like a city. Birds came and went and hopped from bough to bough, twittering importantly of affairs to them important; squirrels scampered over the rough bark, in sudden panic haste, darting little glances, sidewise and behind, after pursuers that (we will hope) were fancied; and other birds, out of sight in the loftier regions, piped their insistent calls, or sang their tireless epithalamiums. Spiders hung in their gossamer lairs, only too tensely motionless not to seem dead; but if a gnat came—with what swift, accurate, and relentless vigour they sprang upon and garotted him. Sometimes a twig snapped, or a young acorn fell, or a caterpillar let himself down by a long silken thread. And the air under the oak was tonic with its good oaken smell.

Susanna was leaning back in a sort of reverie, held by the charm of these things. "We have no trees like this in Italy," she was vaguely thinking. "The trees and the wild creatures are never so near to one there; one never gets so intimate with them; Nature is not so accessible and friendly." She remembered having read somewhere that such enjoyment as she was now experiencing, the enjoyment of commune with the mere sweet out-of-door things of the earth, was a Pagan enjoyment, and un-Christian; and her mind revolted at this, and she thought, "No. There would n't be any enjoyment, if one did n't know that 'God's in His Heaven, all 's right with the world.'"

And just then her reverie was interrupted. . .

"He has arrived. I have seen him—what you call *seen*—with my own eyes seen. There are about two yards of him; and a very spruce, gentlemanlike, well-knit, and attractive two yards they are."

Thus, with a good deal of animation, in a pleasant, crisp old voice, thus spoke Miss Sandus: a little old lady in black: little and very daintily finished, with a daintily-chiselled profile, and a neat, small-framed figure; in a black walking-skirt, that was short enough to disclose a small, high-instepped, but eminently business-like pair of brown boots. Miss Sandus (she gave you her word for it) was seventy-four;—and indeed (so are the generations linked), her father had been a middie with Nelson at Trafalgar, and a lieutenant aboard the *Bellerophon* during that ship's historic voyage to St. Helena;—but she confronted you with the lively eyes, the firm cheeks, the fresh complexion, the erect and active carriage, of a well-preserved woman of sixty; and in her plentiful light-brown hair there was scarcely a thread of grey. She stepped trippingly across the grass, swinging a malacca walking-stick, with a silver crook-handle.

"He has arrived. I 've seen him."

So her voice broke in upon Susanna's musings; and Susanna started, and got up. She was wearing a muslin frock to-day, white, with a pattern of flowers in mauve; and she was without a hat, so that one could see how her fine black hair grew low about her brow, and thence swept away in loose full billows, and little crinkling over-waves, to where it drooped in a rich mass behind. But as she stood, awaiting Miss Sandus's approach, her face was pale, and her eyes were wide open and dark, as if with fright.

"Dear me, child. Did I startle you? I 'm so sorry," said Miss Sandus, coming up to her. "Yes, Don Antonio has arrived. I saw him as he disembarked at his native railway-station. I was ordering a book at Smith's. And such luggage, my dear. Boxes and bags, bags and boxes, till you could n't count them; and all of stout brown leather—so nice and manny. He looks nice and manny himself: tall, with nice manny clothes, and nice eyes, and a nice brown skin; and with a nose, my dear, a nose like Julius Caesar's. Well, you 'll meet him on Sunday, at your Papistical place of worship,—if he does n't call before. I daresay he 'll think himself obliged to."

"Oh, Fairy Godmother," gasped Susanna, faintly; "feel."

She took Miss Sandus's hand, and pressed it against her side.

"Feel how my heart is beating."

"Mercy!" exclaimed Miss Sandus.

IV

"Hang it all, how she sticks in one's mind," said Anthony, with impatience. "Am I returning to my cubhood, that the mere vision of a woman should take possession of me like this?"

And then, having, I suppose, weighed the question, "It's the weather," he decided. "Yes—I 'll bet you ten-and-sixpence that it's nothing more than just this silly, sentimental, languorous June weather."

He was seated in a shaded corner of his garden, where the day was murmurous with the humming of bees, and the mingled sweetness of many flowers rose and fell in the air. Beyond the shade, the sunshine broke into a mosaic of merry colours, on larkspur and iris, pansies and pink geraniums, jessamine, sweet-peas, tulips shameless in their extravagance of green and crimson, red and white carnations, red, white, and yellow roses. The sunshine broke into colour, it laughed, it danced, it almost rioted, among the flowers; but in the prim alleys, and on the formal hedges of box, and the quaintly-clipped yews, and the old purple brick walls, where fruit trees were trellised, it lay fast, fast asleep. Without the walls, in the deep cool greenery of the park, there was a perpetual drip-drip of bird-notes. This was the web, upon which a chosen handful of more accomplished birds were embroidering and cross-embroidering and inter-embroidering their bold, clear arabesques of song. Anthony had a table and a writing-case before him, and was trying to write letters. But now he put down his pen, and, for the twentieth time this afternoon, went over the brief little encounter of the morning.

Two ladies had passed him in a dog-cart, as he was walking home from the village: a young lady driving, an oldish lady beside her, and a groom behind.

That was all: the affair of ten seconds; and at first he was not aware of any deeper or more detailed impression. He had glanced at them vaguely; he was naturally incurious; and he had been thinking of other things.

But by-and-bye, as if his retina had reacted like a photographic plate, a picture developed itself, which, in the end, by a series of recurrences, became quite singularly circumstantial. The dog-cart and its occupants, with the stretch of brown road, and the hedge-rows and meadows at either side, were visible anew to him; and he saw that the young lady who was driving had dark hair and dark eyes, and looked rather foreign; and he said, but without much concern as yet, "Ah, that was no doubt Madame

Torrebianca, with her friend Miss What 's-her-name;"—and proceeded again to think of other things.

The picture faded; but presently it came back. He noticed now that the slightly foreign-looking young woman was pretty, and even interesting-looking; that besides its delicate modelling and its warm, rather Southern colouring, there was character in her face, personality; that there were intelligence, humour, vivacity; that she looked as if she would have something to say. He noticed, too, that she had what they call "a fine figure,"—that she was tall, for a woman, and slender without being thin; that she bore herself well, with an air of strength, with an air of suppleness and resistance. He could even see how she was dressed: in grey cloth, close-fitting, with grey driving-gloves, and a big black hat that carried out the darkness of her hair. And he was intrepid enough to trust his man's judgment, and to formulate an opinion of her dress. She was very well dressed, he ventured to opine; far too cunningly and meticulously dressed for an Englishwoman. There was something of French unity, intention, finish, in her toilet; there was *line* in it, the direct, crisp line, that only foreign women seem anxious to achieve.

And he said, "I rather hope it *is* Madame Torrebianca—since one has got to know her. She looks as if she might have a spice of something in her not utterly banale."

If that was n't saying a great deal, he reflected, one seldom enough, in our staid, our stale society, meets a person of whom one can say so much;—and again dismissed her.

But still again, presently, back she came; and then again and again, in spite of him. And her comings now were preceded by a strange little perturbation. A strange little vague feeling of pleasantness, as if something good had happened to him would begin, and well up, and grow within him, penetrating and intensifying his sense of the summer sweetness round about, till it distracted his attention, and he must suspend his occupation of the moment, to wonder, "What is it?" In response, the vague pleasantness, like a cloud, would draw together and take shape; and there was the spirited grey figure in the dog-cart, with the black hat, and the dark hair and eyes, again dashing past him.

And little by little he discovered that she was more than merely pretty and interesting-looking. Her face, with all its piquancy, was a serious face, a strenuous face. Under its humour and vivacity, he discovered a glow . . . a glow . . . could it be the glow of a soul? Her eyes were lustrous, but they were deep, as well. A quality shone in them rarer even than character: a natural quality, indeed, and one that should naturally be common: but one that is rare in England among women—among nice women, at least: the quality of sex. The woman in the dog-cart was nice. About that, he recognised with instant certainty, there could be no two conjectures. But she was also, he recognised with equal certainty, a woman: the opposite, the complement of man. Her eyes were eyes you could imagine laughing at you, mocking you, teasing you, leading you on, putting you off, seeing through you, disdaining you; but constant in them was the miracle of womanhood; and you could imagine them softening adorably, filling with heavenly weakness, yielding in womanly surrender, trusting you, calling you, needing you.

Our melancholic young squire of Craford was not a man much given to quick-born enthusiasms; but now, as he put down his pen, and her face shone before him for the twentieth time this sunny afternoon, now all at once, "By Jove, she's unique," he cried out. "I have never seen a woman to touch her. If she *is* Madame Torrebianca——"

But there he checked himself.

"Of course she is n't. No such luck," he said, in dejection.

And yet, he speculated, who else could she be? The simultaneous presence of *two* young foreign women in this out-of-the-way country neighbourhood seemed, of all contingencies, the most unlikely. Well, if she really was . . .

He was conscious suddenly of a sensation to the last degree unfamiliar: a commotion, piercing, regretful, desirous, actually in his heart, an organ he had for years proudly fancied immune; and he took alarm.

"Am I eighteen again? Positively, I must not think of her any more."

But it was useless. In two minutes he was thinking of her harder than ever, and the commotion in his heart was renewed.

"If she really is Madame Torrebianca," he told himself, with a thrill and a craving, "I shall see her on Sunday."

The flowers, beyond there, in the sun, the droning of the bees, the liquid bird-notes, the perfumes in the still soft air, all seemed to melt and become part of his thought of her, rendering it more poignant, more insidiously sweet.

At last he started up, in a kind of anger.

"Bah!" he cried, "It's the weather. It's this imbecile, love-sick weather."

And he carried his writing-materials indoors, to the billiard-room, a northern room, looking into the big square court, where the light was colourless, and the only perfume on the air was a ghost-like perfume of last night's tobacco-smoke.

But I don't know that the change did much good. In a few minutes—

"Bah!" he cried again, "It's those confounded eyes of hers. It's those laughing, searching, haunting, promising eyes."

"Bid me discourse, I will enchant thine ear."

It was the voice of Adrian, raised in song. And repeating the same complaisant proffer, to a tune which I suspect was improvised, it drew near along the outer passage, till, in due process, the door of the billiard-room was opened, and Adrian stood upon the threshold.

"Bid me discourse, I will enchant thine e-e-ear," he trolled robustly— and then, espying Anthony, fell silent.

Anthony appeared to be deep engrossed in letter-writing.

"Ahem," said Adrian, having waited a little.

But Anthony did not look up.

"Well, of all unlikely places," said Adrian, wondering.

Anthony's pen flew busily backwards and forwards across his paper.

"Remarkable power of mental concentration," said Adrian, on a key of philosophic comment.

"Eh? What?" Anthony at last questioned, but absently, from the depths, without raising his eyes.

"I 've been hunting far and wide for you—ransacking the house, turning the park topsy-turvy," said Adrian.

"Eh? What?" questioned Anthony, writing on.

But Adrian lost patience.

"Eh? What? I 'll eh-what you," he threatened, shaking his fist. "Come. Put aside that tiresome letter. 'Do you happen to know where your master is?' says I to Wickersmith. 'Well, if you 'll pardon my saying so, sir, I think I see him agoing in the direction of the billiard-room, saving your presence, sir,' says Wickersmith to me." Adrian pantomimed the supposed deference of the butler. Then, loftily, "But, 'Shoo' says I. 'An optical delusion, my excellent Wick. A Christian man would be incapable of such a villainy. The billiard-room, that darksome cavern, on a heaven-sent day like this? Shucks,' says I. Yet"—his attitude became exhortative—"see how mighty is truth, see how she prevails, see how the scoffer is confounded. To the billiard-room I transport myself, sceptically, on the off-chance, and—here, good-lack, you are."

"It's the weather," Anthony explained, having finally relinquished his correspondence. "I was in the garden—but I could n't stand the weather."

"The weather?" wondered Adrian. "You could n't stand the weather? My poor lamb. Ah, what a delicate constitution. He could n't stand the weather." Eyes uplifted, he wagged a compassionate head.

But suddenly, from the sarcastic note, he passed to the censorious, and then to a kind of gay rhapsodic.

"The weather? Shame upon your insinuations. I will not hear one syllable against it. The weather? There never *was* such weather. The weather? Oh, for the tongues of men and angels, to chant the glory of the weather. The weather is made of sugar and spice, of frankincense and myrrh, of milk and honey, of every conceivable ingredient that's nice. The sky is an inverted bowl of Sèvres—that priceless bleu-royal; and there are appetising little clouds of whipped cream sticking to it. The air is full of gold, like eau-de-vie de Dantzic;—if we only had a liquefying apparatus, we could recapture the first fine careless nectar of the gods, the poor dead gods of Greece. The earth is as aromatic as an orange stuck with cloves; I can't begin to tell you all the wondrous woody, mossy, racy things it smells of. The sea is a great sheet of watered-silk, as blue as my blue eyes. And the birds, the robins and the throstles, the blackbirds and the black-caps, the linnets and the little Jenny Wrens, knowing the value of silence, are hoarding it like misers; but like prodigals, they 're squandering sound. The ear of mortal never heard such a delirious, delicious, such a crystalline, argentine, ivory-smooth, velvety-soft, such a ravishing, such an enravished tumult of sweet voices. Showers, cascades, of pearls and rubies, emeralds, diamonds, sapphires. The weather, says Anthony Rowleigh. He could n't stand the weather. The weather is as perfect as a perfect work of art—as perfect as one of my own incomparable madrigals. It is absolutely perfect."

He tossed his head, in sign of finality.

"It appears so," Anthony discriminated gloomily; "but appearances are risky things to judge by. It may have charms for a voluptuary like you; but I"—and he took a tone of high austerity—"I, as an Englishman, have my suspicions of anything so flagrantly un-English."

"Apropos of things un-English," said Adrian, "I 'm pining for a serious word with you."

Anthony pulled a wry face.

"Oh, if you 've been attacked by one of your periodic spasms of seriousness," he sighed.

"It's about calling on Madame Torrebianca," said Adrian.

"Oh," sighed Anthony. With a presence of mind that I can't help thinking rather remarkable, he feigned a continuity of mood; but something went *ping* within him.

"Look here," said Adrian, imperatively. "I 'll thank you to drop that air of ineffable fatigue of yours, and to sit up and listen. I don't suppose you wish to be deliberately discourteous, do you? And as those ladies happen to be new-comers, and your immediate neighbours, not to say your tenants, I expect you are sufficiently acquainted with the usages of polite society to know that a failure on your part to call would be tantamount to a direct affront. Furthermore, as one of them (Miss Sandus is, unhappily, still in the Götterdämmerung of the Establishment), as Madame Torrebianca is coming to your house, as your guest, to hear Mass on Sunday morning, I sincerely hope I need n't tell you that it's simply *de rigueur* that you should call before that occasion."

He stood off, and raised his brown-red eyebrows, as who, from an altitude, speaking *de par le Roi*, should challenge contumacy.

But two could play at the game of eyebrow-raising. Anthony raised his.

"Coming as my guest? Coming as my *guest?* I like that," he exclaimed. "What have *I* to do with her coming? If every stranger to whom you choose to extend the privilege of hearing Mass in the Chapel, is thereby to be constituted a *guest,—my* guest,—I shall have my hands full indeed. If she's a guest at all, if she's anybody's guest, she's yours; You 've created the situation. Don't try to thrust the brunt of it on me."

Adrian flung back his head, and spoke from a still loftier altitude.

"I believe you are the master of the house?"

"The titular master," Anthony distinguished. "I years ago resigned all real power into the pink and chubby hands of my mayor of the palace." And he slightly bowed.

"I disdain to answer your silly quibble over the word *guest*," Adrian continued, ignoring the rejoinder. "La Nobil Donna Susanna Torrebianca is a guest. And as master of the house, by your return, you *ex officio* supersede me in the capacity of host."

"*Ex officio?*" repeated Anthony, considering. "The fashion of adorning ordinary speech with classical quotations has long since passed from use."

"And therefore,"—Adrian brought his theorem to its conclusion,—"unless you particularly aspire to seem—and to be—an absolute barbarian, a bear, a boor, a churl, and a curmudgeon,"—each epithet received an augmented stress,—"you must call at Craford New Manor with the least possible delay. As I find myself in rather good form just now, and feel that I should shine to perhaps exceptional advantage, I suggest that we call forthwith."

Anthony got up, and sleepily stretched his arms.

"Ah, well," he consented; "since your fond heart is set upon it—there. It will be an awful fag; but when Dimplechin becomes importunate, I can deny him nothing."

He stifled a yawn.

Adrian's round face radiated triumph.

"You are a good child, after all," he said, "and you shall have jam with your tea."

"I think I have fooled that fellow to the top of his bent," was Anthony's silent self-gratulation.

His pulse beat high, as they walked across the park.

"How could I ever have contemplated waiting till Sunday?" he asked himself, in a maze.

Sunday, the day after the day after to-morrow, seemed, in his present eagerness, to belong to the dim distances of futurity.

And all the way, as they passed under the great trees, over the cool, close turf, with its powdering of daisies and buttercups and poppies, through alternations of warm sun and deep shadow, where sheep browsed, and little snow-white awkward lambkins sported, and birds piped, and the air was magical with the scent of the blossoming may,—all the way, amid the bright and dark green vistas of lawn and glade, the summer loveliness mixed with his anticipation of standing face to face with her, and rendered it more poignant.

"If cats were always kittens,
And rats were always mice,
And elderberries were younger berries,
Now would n't that be nice?"—

Adrian, walking beside him, trilled joyously.

"You seem in high spirits," Anthony remarked.

"I 've been thinking of your suggestion," said Adrian.

Anthony frowned, at a loss.

"My suggestion—?"

"Yes—your suggestion that I should marry her."

Anthony stared.

"What?" he ejaculated.

"Yes," said Adrian, blandly. "I think the suggestion is decidedly a happy one. I think I shall pay my court to her."

"*You*? Man, you 're bereft of your senses," said Anthony, with force.

"You need n't be so violent," said Adrian. "It's your own idea."

"I was making game of you—I was pulling your leg. Marry her? She would n't look at you," said Anthony, contumelious.

"Why not, I should like to know?" Adrian haughtily enquired.

"You 're—you 're too young," Anthony reminded him.

"Too young?" mildly demurred Adrian, wide-eyed. "I 'm thirty, if I 'm a day."

"You 're thirty-nine, if you 're a day," said Anthony. "But you 'll never be thirty—not even when you 're forty. You breathe perennial spring."

"I confess," said Adrian, with deliberation, "I freely confess that I am not an effete and blasé old thing, like—like one who shall be nameless. There is a variety of fruit (the husbandman's despair), a tough, cross-grained, sour-hearted variety of fruit, that dries up and shrivels, and never ripens. There is another variety of fruit that grows rounder and rosier, tenderer and juicier and sweeter, the longer it hangs on the tree. Time cannot wither it. The child of the sun and the zephyr, it is honey-full and fragrant even unto its inmost ripe red core."

He expanded his chest, and significantly thumped it.

"Mark you," he resumed, "I name no names. The soul of delicacy and discretion, as of modesty and kindness, I name no names. But as for myself, that I am young I acknowledge. Those whom the gods love are ever young. Yet I am old enough, at least, to be capable of fresh, impulsive feelings. I am old enough to have cast the crude, harsh pessimism of inexperience. I am old enough to have outlived my disillusions. I am old enough to have learned that the good things of life are good, and to understand that the rose-buds in the garden are there to be gathered. And I 'm not such a silly as to forbear to gather them. I think I shall make Madame Torrebianca the object of my respectful solicitations."

Anthony fixed eyes of derision on him.

"Oh, the fatuity of the man!" he jeered. "If you could see yourself. You 're sandy-haired—and miles too fat."

"I beg your pardon," said Adrian, with dignity. "My hair is of a very fashionable shade—tawny, which indicates a passionate heart, with under-waves of gold, as if the sunshine had got entangled in it. I will not dwell upon its pretty truant tendency to curl. And as for what you call *fat*—let me tell you that there are people who admire a rich, ample figure in a man. I admit, I am not a mere anatomy, I am not a mere hungry, lean-faced, lantern-jawed, hollow-eyed, sallow-cheeked, vulture-beaked, over-dressed exiguity, like—well, mark you, I name no names. I need not allude to my other and higher attributes—my wit, my sympathy, my charming affectations, my underlying strength of character (a lion clothed in rose-leaves—what?), my genius for the divinest of the arts. I think I shall lay myself at the feet of Donna Susanna. The rest of the sex"—his gesture put them from him—"may coif St. Catherine."

"I have n't the honour of knowing the lady in question," said Anthony, with detachment. "But if she is anything like the paragon you have led me to expect, let me, as your sincere well-wisher, let me warn you not to cherish hopes that are foredoomed to disappointment. If, on the other hand, she should indeed admire your style of rich, ample figure, I shall deem it my duty to save you from her—at no matter what cost to myself. I cannot allow you to link yourself for life to a woman without taste."

And then they rang the bell at the vast, much-bestuccoed portal of the new house; and Anthony's heart, I think, for the minute stood still within him. The door was opened, and he could look into the big, ugly, familiar marble hall;—familiar still, and yet changed and strange, and even beautified; with new soft hangings, and Persian carpets, and flowers, and books, and bibelots about; with a new aspect of luxury and elegance; with a strange new atmosphere of feminine habitation, that went a little to Anthony's head, that called up clearer than ever the dark-haired, strenuous-faced woman of the dog-cart, and turned his imagination to visions and divinings of intimate feminine things. One thought of chiffons, and faint, elusive perfumes, and the gleam and rustle of silken garments; one heard soft voices, trills of feminine laughter, the whispering of feminine secrets; one saw ladies in low chairs, reading or embroidering by lamp-light.

So, for an instant, Anthony stood at Susanna's threshold, looking into her antechamber, breathless almost with his sense of her imminence;—and then the tall flunkey said, in the fastidious accents of flunkeydom, "Net et *em*, sir;" and all my hero's high-strung emotion must spend itself in the depositing of a card.

As they turned away, and the summer landscape again met him with its warm breath and radiant smile, he gloomed at it savagely, from eyes of deep rebuke, as at a thing that had beguiled him with false promises, wronged and defrauded him. And he flew out petulantly at poor Adrian—

"Here's a pretty dance you 've led me, for the pleasure of a word with Mr. Yellowplush."

"Oh?" said Adrian, taken aback. "I expected you 'd be relieved. You did n't want to see them. And the exigencies of the case are satisfied by leaving cards."

"I could have sent my card by you," growled Anthony.

"You 've had a lovely walk, with a lovely comrade, in lovely weather," said Adrian.

"The weather is simply brazen," Anthony declared.

V

Judged by the standards of a cit, countrymen, I believe, are generally early risers; but even for a countryman, Anthony, next morning, rose at an unlikely hour. The tall clock in the hall, accenting with its slow sardonic tick the silence of the sleeping house, marked a quarter to five, as he undid the heavy old-fashioned fastenings of the door, the oaken bar, the iron bolts and chains, and let himself out.

He let himself out; but then he stood still for a minute on the terrace, arrested by the exquisite shock of the wonderful early air: the wonderful light, keen air, a fabric woven of elfin filaments, the breathings of green lives: an aether distilled of secret essences, in the night, by the earth and the sea,—for there was the sea's tang, as well as the earth's balm, there was the bitter-sweet of the sea and the earth at one.

He stood for a minute, stopped by the exquisite shock of it; and then he set forth for an aimless morning ramble.

The dew clung in big iridescent crystals to the grass, where the sheep were already wide-awake and eager at their breakfasts; it gleamed like sprinkled rubies on the scarlet petals of the poppies, and like fairies' draughts of yellow wine in the enamelled hollows of the buttercups; on the brown earth of the pathways, where the long shadows were purple, it lay white like hoar-frost. The shadows were still long, the sunbeams still almost level; the sun shone gently, as through an imperceptible thin veil, gilding with pinkish gold the surfaces it touched—glossy leaves, and the rough bark of tree-trunks, and the points of the spears of grass. A thicker veil, a gauze of pearl and silver, dimmed the blue of the sea, and blurred the architecture of the cliffs. On the sea's edge lay a long grey cloud, a long, low, soft cloud, flat, like a band of soft grey velvet. The cloud was grey indeed; but (as if prismatic fires were smouldering there) its grey held in solution all the colours of the spectrum, so that you could discern elusive rose-tints, fugitive greens, translucent reflections of amethyst and amber.

The morning was inexpressibly calm and peaceful—yet it was busy with sound and with movement. Rooks, those sanctimonious humbugs, circled overhead, cawing thieves' warnings, that had the twang of sermons, to other rooks, out of sight in neighbouring seed-fields. Lapwings, humbugs too, but humbugs in a prettier cause, started from the shrubberies where their eggs were hidden, and fluttered lamely towards the open. Sparrows innumerable were holding their noisy, high-spirited disputations; blackbirds were repeating and repeating that deep melodious love-call of theirs, which they have repeated from the beginning of the world, and no ear has ever tired of; finches were singing, greenfinches, chaffinches; thrushes were singing, singing ecstatically in the tree-tops, and lower down the imitative little blackcaps were trying to imitate them. Recurrently, from a distance, came the soft iterations of a cuckoo. Bees went about their affairs with a mien of sombre resolution, mumbling to themselves, in stolid monotone, "It-'s-got-to-be-done-and-it-'s-dogged-that-does-it, it-'s-got-to-be-done-and-it-'s-dogged-that-does-it," and showing thus that even the beautiful task of flying from flower to flower and gathering honey, may, if you are a bee, fail to interest you, and necessitate an act of will; while butterflies, charmed by the continual surprises, satisfied by the immediate joys, of the present moment, flitted irresponsibly, capriciously, whithersoever a bright colour beckoned, and gave no thought to the moments that had not yet come. Everywhere there was business, rumour, action; but everywhere, none the less, there was the ineffable peace of early morning, of the hours when man—the peace-destroyer?—is still at rest. And everywhere, everywhere, there was the wonderful pristine air, the virginal air, that seemed to penetrate beyond the senses, and to reach the imagination, a voice whispering untranslatable messages, waking mystic surmises of things unknown but somehow kindred.

Anthony strolled on at random, down the purple-shaded paths, under the spreading oaks and bending elms, over the sun-tipped greensward, satisfied, like the butterflies, by the experiences of the passing moment, enjoying, in leisurely intimacy, the aspects and vicissitudes of his way; for a melancholy man, curiously cheerful; the tears of things, the flat and unprofitable uses of the world, forgotten: for a melancholy man, even curiously elated: elated—oh, more than likely without recognising it—as one is to whom the house of life has discovered a new chamber-door, and, therewith, new promises of adventure. He strolled on at random, swinging his stick nonchalantly, . . . till, all at once, he saw something that brought him, and the heart within him, to a simultaneous standstill: something he had been more or less sub-consciously thinking of the whole time, perhaps?—for it brought him to a standstill, as if he saw his thought made flesh.

He had just mounted a little knoll, and now, glancing down before him, he saw, not twenty yards away, under a hawthorn in full blossom,—

"Madame Torrebianca, as I am alive," he gasped.

VI

Susanna was standing under the tree, gazing intently upwards; and she was vehemently shaking her fist at its foliage, and making, from the point of her lips, a sound, sibilant, explosive (something like "Ts-s-s! Ts-s-s-s! Ts-s-s-s-s!"), that was clearly meant as an intimidation. She had on a dark-blue frock, blue flannel I think, plain to the verge of severity: a straight-falling jacket, a straight, loose skirt: plain, but appropriate to the hour no doubt; and, instead of a hat, she wore a scarf of black lace, draped over her black hair mantilla-wise.

Anthony, glowing with a sense that he was in great luck, and trying to think what practical step he should take to profit by it, watched her for a minute before she caught sight of him. An obvious practical step, she having evidently some trouble on her hands, might have been to approach her with an offer of assistance. But if all who love are poets, men near to love will be poets budding; and who was it said that the obvious is the one thing a poet is incapable of seeing?

When, however, she did catch sight of him, abruptly, without hesitation, she called him to her.

"Come here—come here at once," she called, and made an imperious gesture. (I wonder whether she realised who he was, or thought no further as yet, in her emergency, than just that here, providentially, was a man who could help.)

Marvelling, palpitating, Anthony flew to obey.

"Look," said Susanna, breathlessly, pointing into the tree. "What is one to do? He won't pay the slightest attention to me, and I have nothing that I can throw."

She had, in her left hand, a small leather-bound book, apparently a prayer-book, and, twisted round her wrist, a red-coral rosary; but I suppose she would not have liked to throw either of these.

Bewildered a little by the suddenness with which the situation had come to pass, but conscious, acutely, exultantly conscious of it as a delectable situation,—exultantly conscious of her nearness to him, of their solitude together, there in the privacy (as it were) of the morning,—and tingling to the vibrations of her voice, to the freshness and the warmth of her strong young beauty, Anthony was still able, vaguely, half-mechanically, to lift his eyes, and look in the direction whither she pointed. . .

The spectacle that met him banished immediately, for the moment, all preoccupations personal.

On one of the lower of the flowering branches, but high enough to be beyond arm's reach, or even cane's reach, in the crook of the bough, crouched, making ready to spring, a big black cat, the tip of his tail twitching with contained excitement, his yellow eyes fixed murderously on the branch next above: where, in the agitation of supreme distress, a chaffinch, a little grey hen-chaffinch, was hopping backwards and forwards, sometimes rising a few inches into the air, but always returning to the branch, and uttering a succession of terrified, agonised, despairing tweets.

It was a hateful thing to see. It was the genius of cruelty made manifest in a single intense tableau.

"Why does n't the bird fly away?" Susanna painfully questioned. She was pale, and her lips were strained; she looked sick and hopeless. "Is she fascinated? The cat will surely get her."

"No—her nest must be somewhere there—she is guarding her nestlings," said Anthony.

Then he raised his stick menacingly, and, in tones of stern command, addressed the cat.

"Patapouf! I am ashamed of you. Come down—come down from there—come down directly."

And he emphasised each staccato summons by a sharp rap of his stick against the highest point of the tree that he could reach.

The cat turned his head, to look—and the spell was broken. His attitude relaxed. Anthony put his hands on the tree, and made as if to climb it. The cat gave a resigned shrug of the shoulders, and came scrambling down. Next instant, (if you please), unabashed, tail erect, back arched, he was rubbing his whiskers against Anthony's legs, circling round them, s-shaping himself between them, and purring conciliations, as who should say, "There, there. Though you *have* spoiled sport, I won't quarrel with you, and I *am* delighted to see you." The bird, twittering, flew up, and disappeared in the higher foliage.

Susanna breathed a deep sigh of relief.

"Oh, thank you, thank you," she said, with fervour. Then she shook her finger, and frowned, at Patapouf. "Oh, you bad cat! You cruel cat!" And raising eyes dark with reproach to Anthony's, "Yet he seems to be a friend of yours?" she wondered. (By this time, of course, she must have realised who he was. Very likely she had her emotions.)

Anthony, the bird in safety, could tingle anew to the deep notes of her voice, could exult anew in their dual solitude.

"Yes," he acknowledged, "Patapouf is a friend of mine—he is even a member of my household. You must try not to think too ill of him. He really is n't half a bad sort at bottom. But he 's English, and he lives in the country. So, a true English country gentleman, he has perhaps an exaggerated passion for the pleasures of the chase—and when questions touching them arise, seems simply to be devoid of the ethical sense. He 's not a whit worse than his human neighbours—and he 's a hundred times handsomer and more intelligent."

Susanna, smiling a little, looked down at Patapouf, and considered.

"He is certainly very handsome," she agreed. "And—Patapouf? I like his name. I will not think too ill of him if he will promise never again to try to catch a—a *fringuello*. I don't remember the English for *fringuello*?"

Her glance and her inflection conveyed a request to be reminded.

But Anthony shook his head.

"And I shall at once proceed to forget it. *Fringuello* is so much prettier."

Susanna gave a light little trill of laughter.

"What a delicious laugh," thought he that heard it.

And, laughing, "But before it has quite gone from you, do, pray, for my instruction, just pronounce it once," she pleaded.

"How extraordinarily becoming to her that mantilla is," he thought. "How it sets off her hair and her complexion—how it brings out the sparkle of her eyes."

Her fine black hair, curling softly about her brow, and rippling away, under the soft black lace, in loose abundance; her warm, clear complexion; the texture of her skin, firm and smooth, with tiny blue veins faintly showing at the temples; her sparkling, spirited dark eyes, their merriment, their alertness, their graver underglow; the spirited, high carriage of her head; that dark-blue, simple, appropriate frock; and then her figure, upright, nervous, energetic, with its fluent lines, with its fragrance of youth and of womanhood,—oh, he was acutely conscious of them, he was thrilled by his deep sense of their nearness to him, alone there, in the wide sunny circle of green landscape, in the seclusion of that unfrequented hour.

"The word comes back to me dimly," he said, "as—as something like *finch*."

"Finch?" said Susanna. "Thank you very much. Ah, yes,"—with an air of recalling it,—"*finch*, to be sure. You are right," she smiled, "*fringuello* is prettier."

"What an adorable mouth," thought he. "The red of it—the curves it takes—and those incredible little white teeth, like snow shut in a rose."

"And this is a morning meet for pretty words, is it not?" he suggested. "It might strike an unprejudiced observer as rather a pretty morning."

"Oh, I should be less reticent," said Susanna. "If the unprejudiced observer had his eyes open, would n't it strike him as a perfectly lovely morning?"

"We must not run the risk of spoiling it," Anthony cautioned her, diminishing his voice, "by praising it too warmly to its face."

She gave another light trill of laughter.

"Her laugh is like rainbow-tinted spray. It is a fountain-jet of musical notes, each note a cut gem," thought the infatuated fellow.

"I trust," he hazarded, "that you will not condemn me for a swaggerer, if I lay claim to share with you a singularity. The morning is a morning like another. God is prodigal of lovely mornings. But we two are singular in choosing to begin it at its sweeter end."

"Yes," Susanna assented, "that is a singularity—in England. But in Italy, or in the part of Italy where my habits were formed, it is one of our lazy customs. We like always to be abroad in time to enjoy what we call 'the hours immaculate,'—*l'ure immacolae*, in our dialect."

"The hours immaculate? It is an uncommonly fine description," approved
Anthony. "They will be a race of poets in your part of Italy?"

The graver underglow in Susanna's eyes eclipsed, for an instant, their dancing surface lights.

"They *were* a race of poets," she said regretfully, "before they learned how to read and write. But now, with the introduction of popular education,"—she shook her head,—"the poetry is dying out."

"Ah," said Anthony, with a meaning flourish of his stick, "there it is. The poetic spirit always dies at the advance of that ghastly fetich." Then he spoke sententiously. "Popular education is a contrivance of the devil, whereby he looks to extinguish every last saving grace from the life of the populace. Not poetry only, but all good things and all good feelings,—religion, reverence, courtesy,—sane contentment, rational ambition,—the right sort of humility, the right sort of pride,—they all go down before it: whilst, in the ignorance which it disseminates, blasphemy, covetousness, bumptiousness, bad taste (and bad art and bad literature, to gratify it), every form of wrong-headedness and wrong-heartedness flourish like the seven plagues of Egypt. But it was all inevitable from the day that meddling German busybody invented printing—if not from the day his heathenish precursor invented letters."

He delivered these sentiments with a good deal of warmth.

Susanna's eyes brightened. I am not sure there was n't a quick little flash of raillery in their brightness.

"I would seem," she mused, "to have touched by accident upon a subject that is near your heart."

Anthony threw up a deploring hand.

"There!" he grieved. "The subjects that are near my heart, it is the study of my life to exclude from my conversation. But sometimes one forgets oneself."

Susanna smiled,—a smile, perhaps, that implied a tacit memorandum and reflection, a subdued, withheld, occult little smile. Again, I am not sure it had n't its tinge of raillery.

"And since I *have* forgotten myself," Anthony pursued, "I wonder whether you will bear with me if I continue to do so twenty seconds longer?"

"Oh, I beg of you," Susanna politely hastened to accede.

"There is another subject equally near my heart," said he.

Her eyes were full of expectancy.

"Yes—?" she encouraged him.

"I was disappointed not to find you at home when I called yesterday," said he. "I rejoice for a hundred reasons that chance has led to our meeting this morning. Not to mention ninety-nine of them, I am anxious to discharge, with as little loss of time as may be, the very onerous debt I owe you."

Susanna opened her eyes, in puzzlement.

"A debt? I am your creditor unawares."

"My debt of apologies and condolences," he explained.

She knitted her brows, in mental effort.

"I am ignorant alike of my grievance and of your offence," she said.

"I am deeply sensible of your magnanimity," said he; "but I will not abuse it. They have let you the ugliest house in the United Kingdom; and, as the owner, the ultimate responsibility must come home to me."

"Oh," cried Susanna.

It was a gay, treble little cry, that told him he had been fortunate enough to amuse as well as to surprise her. She shook her head, while her eyes were liquid with mirth.

"The house is ugly?" she enquired. "I have read of it as 'a vast and imposing edifice in the style of the Renaissance.'"

"As a confessor of the True Faith," Anthony warned her, "you must never believe what you read in the *County History*. It was compiled by a Protestant clergyman; it teems with misinformation; it ought to be placed upon the Index. The house in question is a vast and pompous contiguity of stucco, in the style of 1830. It looks like a Riviera hotel a good deal run to seed. It looks like a shabby relation of Buckingham Palace. It looks like a barrack decorated with the discoloured trimmings of a bride-cake."

"Ah, well, be it so," consented Susanna. "The house is ugly—but it is comfortable. And, in any case, your conscience is too sensitive. The ultimate responsibility for my having taken it comes home to no one, unless—well, to be strictly just, unless to a grandfather of mine, who has been dead these many long years."

Which pronouncement may very possibly have struck her listener as enigmatic. But I daresay he felt that he scarcely knew her well enough to press for an elucidation. And, anyhow, without pause, she went on—

"Besides, everything else—the park, the country—is beyond words beautiful."

"Yes," acquiesced Anthony, "the country is beautiful, at this season. That's why everyone abandons it, and scuttles up to town."

Susanna's face lighted, with interest.

"Indeed? Is *that* the reason? I had observed the fact, but I was at a loss to think what the reason for it could be."

"No," said Anthony, eating his words, "that is not the reason. It were base to deceive you. A normally-constituted Englishman no more objects to beauty, than a deep-sea fish objects to dry weather or the income-tax. He abandons the country during the three pleasantest months of the year, not because it is beautiful, for he is sublimely unconscious that it's beautiful, but because, during those months, in the country, there's nothing that he can course, hunt, or shoot."

Susanna pondered.

"I see," she said. "And is—is there anything that he can course, hunt, or shoot in town?"

"Not exactly," Anthony admitted. "But there are people—to whom he can do the next best thing. There are people whom he can bore. It is an interim sport. It is an annual national tournament. The good knights flock together from the four corners of England, to tilt at one another, and try who shall approve himself the most indefatigable, the most indomitable bore."

Susanna gazed dreamily at the distance for a moment. Then, with sudden actuality, "Apropos of interim sports," she demanded, "what are you going to do about that cat of yours?" A movement of her head indicated Patapouf.

Hovering near them, Patapouf was busy with a game of make-believe—pretending that the longish grass was a jungle, and himself a tiger, stalking I know not what visionary prey: now gingerly, with slow calculated liftings and down-puttings of his feet, stealing a silent march; now, flat on his belly, rapidly creeping forward; now halting, recoiling, masking himself behind some inequality of the ground, peering warily over it, while his tail swayed responsive to the eager activity of his brain; and now, having computed the range to a nicety, his haunches wagging, now, with a leap all grace and ruthlessness,—a flash of blackness through the air,—springing upon the creature of his fancy.

Susanna and Anthony watched him for a little without speaking.

"You can't deny that he has imagination," said Anthony, at length, turning towards her.

"He is beautiful and clever," said Susanna, "I could wish he were as virtuous. This, of course, is sheer play-acting. He 's simply waiting till our backs are turned, to renew his designs upon the bird's nest."

"When I turn my back I 'll carry him with me," Anthony answered. But in his soul he said: "What 's the good of telling her that that will only be to defer the evil moment? Of course he has marked the tree. He will come back to it at his leisure."

"I beg your pardon," said Susanna. "That will merely be to put the evil off. The cat certainly knows the tree. Directly he 's at liberty, he will come back."

"Oh—?" faltered Anthony, a trifle disconcerted. "Oh? Do—do you think so?"

"Yes," she said. "There 's not a doubt of it. But I am acquainted with a discipline, which, if I have your sanction to apply it, will unnerve Monsieur Patapouf, so far as this particular tree is concerned, until the end of time. Cats have a very high sense of their personal freedom—they hate to be tied up. Well, if we tie Monsieur Patapouf to this tree, so that he can't get away, and leave him alone here for an hour or two, he will conceive such a distaste for everything connected with this tree that he will never voluntarily come within speaking distance of it again."

"Really? That seems very ingenious," commented Anthony.

"'T is an old wives' remedy," said Susanna. "You don't happen to have such a thing as a piece of string in your pocket? It does n't matter. But you have a penknife? Thank you. Now please catch your cat."

Anthony called Patapouf, exerting those blandishments one must exert who would coax a hesitating cat.

Patapouf, by a series of étapes and délours, approached, and was secured.

Susanna, meanwhile, having laid her rosary and prayer-book on the grass, unbuttoned her blue flannel jacket, and removed from round her waist, where it was doing duty as a belt, a broad band of cherry-coloured ribbon. This, with Anthony's penknife, she slitted and ripped several times lengthwise, till she had obtained a yard or two of practicable tether.

"Now, first, we must make him a collar," she said, measuring off what she deemed ribbon sufficient for that purpose.

Anthony held Patapouf, who, flattered by their attentions, and unsuspicious of their ulterior aim, submitted quietly, while Susanna adjusted the collar to his neck. They had to stand rather close together during this process; I am not sure that sometimes their fingers did n't touch. From Susanna's garments—from her hair?—rose never so faint a perfume, like the perfume of violets. I am quite sure that Anthony's heart was in a commotion.

"There," she remarked, finishing the collar with a bow, and bestowing upon the bow a little tap of approbation; "red and black—it's very becoming to him, is n't it?"

Then she tied Patapouf to the tree, leaving him, in charity, perhaps twice his own length of tether free, and resumed possession of her book and beads.

An instant later, she had slightly inclined her head, smiled a good-bye into Anthony's eyes, and was moving briskly away, in the direction of Craford New Manor.

VII

Adrian, pink with the livelier pink of Adrian freshly tubbed and razored, and shedding a cheerful aroma of bay-rum, regarded Anthony, across the bowlful of roses that occupied the centre of the breakfast table, with a show of perplexity.

In the end, thrusting forward his chin, and dropping his eyelids, whereby his expression became remote and superior, "The state of mind of a person like you," he announced, "is a thing I am totally unable to conceive."

And he plunged his spoon into his first egg.

"It is inexplicable, it is downright uncanny," Anthony was thinking, as he munched his toast, "the effect she produces upon a man; the way she pursues one, persists with one. I see her, I hear her voice, her laughter, as clearly as if she were still present. I can't get rid of her, I can't shut her out."

Adrian, his announcement provoking no response, spoke up.

"I am utterly unable," he repeated, "to conceive the state of mind of a person like you."

"Of course you are," said Anthony, with affability.

"I suppose," he thought, "it's because she is what they call a pronounced personality,—though that does n't seem a very flattering description. I suppose it's her odylic force."

Adrian selected a second egg, and placed it in his egg-cup.

"You live, you move, you have a sort of being," he said, as he operated upon the egg-shell; "and, apparently, you live contented. Yet, be apprised by me, you live in the manner of the beasts that perish. For the whole excuse, warrant, purpose, and business of life, you treat as alien to your equation."

"The business of life I entrust to my eminently competent man of business," said Anthony, with a bow.

"She 's so magnificently vivid," he thought. "That white skin of hers, and the red lips, and the white teeth; that cloud of black hair, and the sweep of it as it leaves her brow; and then those luminous, lucid, glowing, glowing eyes—that last smile of them, before she went away! She gives one such a sense of intense vitality, of withheld power, of unknown possibilities."

Adrian, with some expenditure of pains, extracted the spine from a grilled sardine.

"These children of the inconstant wave," he mused, "these captives from the inscrutable depths of ocean—the cook ought to bone them before she sends them to table, ought n't she? *Labor et amor.* The warrant for life is labour, and the business of life is love."

"You should address your complaints to the cook in person," said Anthony.

"That's it—unknown possibilities," he thought. "She 's vivid, but she is n't obvious. It's a vividness that is all reserves—that hints, but does n't tell. It's the vividness of the South, of the Italy that produced her,—'Italy, whose work still serves the world for miracle.' She's vivid, but not in primary colours. I defy you, for example, to find the word for her—the word that would make her visible to one who had never seen her."

"They 're immensely improved by a drop or two of Worcester sauce," said Adrian, with his mouth full. "Observe how, in the labyrinth of destiny, journeys end in the most romantic and improbable conjunctions. These fishlets from a southern sea—this sauce from a northern manufacturing town."

"And then her figure," thought Anthony; "that superb, tall, pliant figure,—the flow of it, the spring of it,—the lines it takes when she moves, when she walks,—its extraordinary union of strength with fineness."

"The longest night," said Adrian, "is followed by a dawn." He dropped three lumps of sugar into his tea-cup. "There 's a paragraph in this week's *Beaux and Belles* which says that sugar in tea is quite the correct thing again. Thank mercy. Tongue can never tell the hankerings my sweet-tooth has suffered during the years that sugar has been unfashionable.

"Nearest neighbours though they dwell,
Neighbour Tongue can never tell
What Neighbour Tooth has had to dree,
Nearest neighbours though they be,"

he softly hummed. "But that's really from a poem about toothache, and does n't perhaps apply. Do *you* labour? Do *you* love?" he enquired.

"Love is such an ambiguous term," said Anthony, with languor.

"Yes—strength and fineness: those are her insistent notes," he was thinking. "She is strong, strong. She is strong as a perfect young animal is strong. Yet she is fine. She is fine as only, of all created beings, a fine woman can be fine—a woman delicate, sensitive, high-bred, fine in herself, and with all her belongings fine."

"Life," said Adrian, "is a thing a man should come by honestly; a thing the possession of which a man should justify; a thing a man should earn."

"Some favoured individuals, I have heard, inherit it from their forebears," said Anthony, as one loth to dogmatise, on the tone of a mere suggestion.

"Pish," answered Adrian, with absoluteness. "Our forebears affect my thesis only in so far as they did not forbear. At most, they touched the button. The rest—the adventurous, uncertain, interesting rest—we must do ourselves. We must *earn* our life; and then we should *spend* it—lavishly, like noble, freehanded gentlemen. Well, we earn our life by labour; and then, if we spend as the gods design, we spend our life in love. I could quote Browning, I could quote Byron, I could even quote What's-his-name, the celebrated German."

"You could—but you won't," interposed Anthony, with haste. "It is excellent to have a giant's strength, but tyrannous to use it like a giant."

"The puzzling thing, however," he reflected, "is that I can't in the least realise her as what she is. She is a widow, she has been married. I can't in the least think of her as a woman who has been married. Not that she strikes one exactly as a young girl, either,—she exhibits too plentiful a lack of young-girlish rawness and insipidity,—she's a woman, she's a *femme faite*. But I can't think of her as a woman who has passed through marriage. One feels a freshness, a bloom, a something untouched, intact. One feels the presence of certain inexperiences. And yet—well, by the card, one's feeling is mistaken."

Adrian sprinkled sugar and poured cream over a plateful of big red strawberries.

"All this—and Heaven too," he piously murmured.

Then, rosy face and blue eyes bright with anticipation, he tasted one. Slowly the brightness faded.

"Deceivers!" he cried, falling back in his seat, and shaking his fist at the tall glass dish from which he had helped himself. "Fair as Hyperion, false as dicers' oaths. Acid and watery—a mere sour bath. You may have them all." He pushed the dish towards Anthony. "I suppose it's too early in the season to hope for good ones. But this"—he charged a plate with bread, butter, and marmalade—"this honest, homely Scottish marmalade, this can always be depended upon to fill the crannies." And therewith he broke into song.

"To fill the crannies,
The mannie's crannies,

Then hey for the sweeties of bonny Dundee!" he carolled lustily. "Let me see—I was saying?" he resumed. "Ah, yes, I was saying that the state of mind of a man like you is a thing I am utterly unable to conceive. And that 's funny, because it is generally true that the larger comprehends the less. But I look at you, and I think to myself, thinks I, 'There is a man—or at least the semblance of a man,—a breathing thing at least, with anthropoid features and dimensions,—who is never, never, never tormented by the feeling—'Now, tell me, what feeling do you conjecture I mean?"

"Don't know, I 'm sure," said Anthony, without much animation.

"'By the feeling that he ought to be bending over a sheet of paper, ruled in pretty parallels of fives, trying to embellish the same with semi-breves and crotchets.' That is what I think to myself, thinks I; and the thought leaves me gasping. I am utterly unable to conceive your state of mind."

"I shan't—barring happy accidents—see her again till Sunday; and to-day is only Friday," Anthony was brooding.

"Apropos," he said to Adrian, "I remember your telling me that Friday was unlucky."

"Tut," said Adrian. "That is n't apropos in the slightest degree. The difference that baffles me, I expect, is that I 've the positive, you 've the negative, temperament; I 've the active, you 've the passive; I 've the fertile, you 've the sterile. It's the difference between Yea and Nay, between Willy and Nilly. Serenely, serenely, you will drift to your grave, and never once know what it is to be consumed, harried, driven by a deep, inextinguishable, unassuageable craving to write a song. You 'll never know the heartburn, the unrest, the conscience-sickness, the self-abasement that I know when I 'm not writing one, nor the glorious anguish of exhilaration when I am. I can get no conception of your state of mind—any more than a nightingale could conceive the state of mind of a sparrow. In a sparrowish way, it must be rather blissful—no? We artists are the salt of the earth, of course; but every art knows its own bitterness, and—*il faut souffrir pour être sel.*"

"It's the difference between egotism rampant and modesty regardant," Anthony, with some grimness, returned. "I am content to sit in my place, and watch the pantomime. You long to get upon the stage. Your unassuageable craving to write a song is, in its essence, just an unassuageable craving to make yourself an object of attention. And that's the whole truth about you artists. I recollect your telling me that Friday was unlucky."

"Oh, how superficial you are," Adrian plaintively protested. "A man like me, you should understand, is meant for the world—for the world's delight, for mankind's wonder. And here unfortunate circumstances—my poverty and not my will—constrain me to stint the world of its due: to languish in this lost corner of Nowhere, like Wamba the son of Witless, the mere professed buffoon of a merer franklin. Well, my unassuageable craving to write a song is, in its essence, just a great, splendid, generous desire to indemnify the world. The world needs me—the world has me not—but the world *shall* have me. For the world's behoof, I will translate myself into semi-breves and crotchets. So *there*! Besides, to be entirely frank, I can't help it. Nothing human is perfect that does not exhibit somewhere a fine inconsequence. Thus I exhibit mine. I make music from a high sense of duty, to enrich the world; but at the same time I make it because I can't help making it. I make it as the bee makes honey, as the Jew makes money, spontaneously, inevitably. It is my nature to,—just as it 's the nature of fire to burn, and of dairy-maids to churn. It is the inherent, ineradicable impulse of my bounteous soul."

"You told me in so many words that Friday was unlucky," said Anthony.

"Well, and so it is," said Adrian.

"I don't agree with you. Friday, in my experience, is the luckiest day of the seven. All sorts of pleasant things have happened to me on Friday."

"That's merely because your sponsors in baptism happened to name you Tony," Adrian explained. "Friday, and the still more dread thirteen, are both lucky for people who happen to be named Tony. Because why? Because the blessed St. Anthony of Padua was born on a Friday, and went to his reward on a thirteenth—the thirteenth of June, this very month, no less." He allowed Anthony's muttered "*A qui le dites-vous?*" to pass unnoticed, and, making his voice grave, continued, "But for those of us who don't happen to be named Tony—*unberufen*! Take a man like me, for instance, an intellectual young fellow, with work to do, but delicate, and dependent for his strength upon the regular administration of sustaining nourishment. Well, Friday comes, and there he is, for twenty-four hours by the clock, obliged to keep up, as best he may, on fish and vegetables and suchlike kickshaws, when every fibre of his frame is crying out for meat, red meat. And now"—he pushed back his chair—"and now, dear heart, be brave. Steel yourself to meet adversity. A sorrow stoically borne is already half a sorrow vanquished. I must absent thee from thy felicity a while——I must be stepping." He rose, and moved, with that dancing gait of his, to the door. From the threshold he remarked, "If you will come to my business-room about half an hour before luncheon, I shall hope to have the last bars polished off, and I 'll sing you something sweeter than ever plummet sounded. *Lebe wohl.*"

"Yes," thought Anthony, left to himself, "barring happy accidents, I must wait till Sunday."

And he went into the park.

"The nuisance," he said to Patapouf, as he released him, "the nuisance of things happening early is that they 're just so much the less likely to happen late. The grudge I bear the Past is based upon the circumstance that it has taken just so much from the Future. Meanwhile, suggest the unthinking, let's enjoy the present. But virtually, as I need n't remind *you*, there is no such thing as the present. The present is an infinitesimal between two infinites. 'T is a line (a thing without breadth or thickness) moving across the surface of Eternity. The present is no more, by the time you have said, This is present. So, then, it were inordinate to hope to fall in with her again to-day, and you and I must face an anti-climax. Be thankful we have the memories of the morning to feed upon. And, if you desire a subject for meditation, observe how appetites are created. If we had not met her at all, we should not hunger and thirst in this way for another meeting."

He left the red collar round Patapouf's neck. The rest of the torn ribbon he carefully gathered up and put in his pocket-book.

VIII

"One should, however, give happy accidents a certain encouragement," he reflected, as he woke next morning. "She said it was her habit. We will seek her again in the hours immaculate."

He sought her far and near. He wandered the park till breakfast time. The appropriate scene was set: the familiar sheep were there, the trees, the birds, the dewy swards, the sunshine and the shadows: but—though, at each new turning, as each new prospect opened, expectancy anew looked eagerly from his eyes—the lady of the piece was ever missing.

"And yet you boasted it was your habit," bitterly he reproached his vision of her.

All day he held out to happy accidents what encouragement he might. All day he roamed the park, and, as the day dragged on, became a deeply dejected man. Even the certitude of seeing her to-morrow was of small comfort.

"Two minutes before Mass, and three minutes after—what is that?" he grumbled.

Towards five o'clock he took a resolution.

"There are such things as accidents, but there is also," he argued, "such a thing as design. Why is man endowed with free-will? I don't care how it may look, nor what they may think. I 'm going to call upon her, I 'm going to ask myself to tea."

In this, however, he reckoned without the keeper of her door.

"The ladies er *ait*, sir," announced that prim-lipped functionary.

"Now farewell hope," he mourned, as the door closed in his face. "There's nothing left for me to do but to go for a thundering long walk, and tire myself into oblivion. I will walk to Wetherleigh."

Head bent, eyes downcast, sternly resolved to banish her from his thought, he set forwards, with rapid, dogged steps. He had gone, it may be, a hundred yards, when a voice stopped him.

"Sh—sh! Please—please!" it whispered.

IX

The grounds immediately appertaining to Craford New Manor are traversed by a brook. Springing from amidst a thicket of creepers up the hillside, it comes tumbling and winding, a series of miniature cascades, over brown rocks, between mossy banks shadowed by ferns and eglantine, through the sun-shot dimness of a grove of pine-trees, to fling itself with a final leap and flash (such light-hearted self-immolation) into the ornamental pond at the bottom of the lawn. It is a pretty brook, and pleasing to the ear, with its purl and tinkle of crisp water.

And now, as Anthony, heading for the Wetherleigh-wards exit of the park, approached the brook, to cross it,—"Sh, sh—please, please,"—a whisper stopped him.

There by the bank, under the tall pines, where sun and shadow chequered the russet carpet of pine-needles, there, white-robed, sat Susanna: white-robed, hatless, gloveless. She was waving her hand, softly, in a gesture invocative of caution; but her eyes smiled a welcome to him.

Anthony halted, waited,—his heart, I think, high-bearing.

"It is a blue tit," she explained, under her breath, eagerly. "The rarest bird that ever comes. He is bathing—there—see." She pointed.

Sure enough, in a little rock-formed pool a couple of yards up-stream, a tiny blue titmouse was vigorously enjoying his bath—ducking, fluttering, preening his plumage, ducking again, and sending off shooting-stars of spray, prismatic stars where they crossed the sunbeams.

"That is the delight of this bit of water," Susanna said, always with bated breath. "The birds for miles about come here to drink and bathe. All the rarer and timider birds, that one never sees anywhere else."

"Ah, yes. Very jolly, very interesting," said Anthony, not quite knowing what he said, perhaps, for his faculties, I hope, were singing a *Te Deum*. But—with that high nose of his, that cool grey eye, with that high collar too, and the general self-assurance of his toilet—no one could have appeared more composed or more collected.

"You speak without conviction," said Susanna. "Don't you care for birds?"

("Come! You must get yourself in hand," his will admonished his wit.)

"I beg your pardon," he said, "I care for them very much. They 're an indispensable feature of the landscape, and immensely serviceable to the agriculturist. But one cares for other things as well. And I had always fancied that the crowning virtue of this bit of water (since you mention it) was its amenability to the caprice of man."

"Men *have* caprices?" questioned she, surprise in her upward glance.

"At any rate," he answered, with allowance for her point, "your Scottish gardener has. At his caprice, he turns this torrent on or off, with a tap. For all its air of naturalness and frank impetuosity, it is an entirely artificial torrent; and your Scottish gardener turns it on and off with a tap."

"He sways the elements," murmured Susanna, as with awe. "Portentous being." Then, changing her note to one of gaiety, "*Ecco*," she cried, "Signor Cinciallegra has completed his ablutions—and *ecco*, he flies away. Won't you—won't you sit down?" she asked, as her eyes came back from the departing bird; and a motion of her hand made him free of the pine-needles.

"Thank you," responded Anthony, taking a place opposite her. "I 'm not sure," he added, "whether in honesty I ought n't to confess that I have just been calling upon you."

"Oh," she said, with the politest smile and bow. "I am so sorry to have missed your visit."

"You are very good." He bowed in his turn. "I wanted to consult you about a trifling matter of business," he informed her.

"A matter of business—?" she wondered; and her face became all attention.

"Exactly," said he. "I wanted to ask what you meant by stating that it was your habit always to be abroad in the hours immaculate? I happened by the merest chance to be abroad in them myself this morning. I examined every nook and cranny of them, I turned them inside out; but not one jot or tittle of you could I discover."

Susanna's eyes were pensive.

"I was speaking of Italy, was I not?" she replied. "I said, I think, that it was the habit of the people in my part of Italy. But, anyhow, one sometimes varies one's habits. And, after all, one sometimes makes statements that are rash."

"And one is always free to repudiate one's responsibilities," suggestively supplemented our young man.

"Fortunately," she agreed. "Moreover," she changed her ground, "one should not be too exclusive in one's sympathies, one should not be unfair to other hours. This present hour here now—is it not immaculate also? With its pure sky, and its odour of warm pines, its deep cool shadows, its patines of bright gold where the sun penetrates, and then, plashing through it, this curling, dimpling, artificial torrent? It is not the hour's fault if it happens to arrive somewhat late in the day—it had to wait its turn. Besides, if one can believe what one reads in books, it will be the very earliest of early hours—down there," (with the tip of a vertical finger she touched the earth), "at the Antipodes."

"To this present hour," said Anthony, with impressive slowness, "I personally owe so great a debt of thankfulness, it would be churlish of me even to hint a criticism. And yet—and yet—how shall I express it? *Eppur' si muove.* It moves, it hastes away;—while I could wish it to remain forever, fixed as the Northern Star. Do they know, in your part of Italy, any means by which the sparkling minutes can be prevailed upon to stay their flight?"

"That is a sort of knowledge," Susanna answered, with a movement of the head, "for which, I fear, one would have to go to a meta-physical and thrifty land like Germany. We are not in the least metaphysical or thrifty in my part of Italy. We allow the sparkling minutes to slip between our fingers, like gold between the fingers of a spendthrift. But—but we rather enjoy the feeling, as they slip."

"I wonder," Anthony hazarded, "whether you would take it very much amiss if—if I should make a remark?"

Susanna's eyes lighted, dangerously.

"I wonder," she said, on a key of dubious meditation.

"I am not easily put off," said he, with firmness. "I am moved to remark upon the astonishing facility with which you speak English. Now—do your worst."

Susanna smiled.

"It would take more than that to provoke me to do my worst," she said. "English is as natural to me as my mother-tongue. I always had English governesses. Everyone has English governesses in Italy nowadays, you know."

"Yes," he said, "I know; and they are generally Irish, are they not? Of course you 've lived a great deal in England?" he surmised.

"On the contrary," she set him right, "this is my first visit here."

"Is it possible?" he marvelled. "I thought the true Oxford accent could only be acquired on the spot."

"Have I the true Oxford accent?" Susanna brightly doubted, eye-brows raised.

"Thank heaven," he gravely charged her, "thank heaven, kneeling, that you have n't the true Oxford manner. Does England," he asked, "seem very rum?"

"Yes," she answered, with immediate candour, "England seems very rum—but not so rum as it might, perhaps, if I had n't read so many English novels. English novels are the only novels you 're allowed to read, in my part of Italy, when you 're young."

"Ah," said Anthony, nodding, "that's because our English novelists are such dabs at the art of omission." And after the briefest pause, "Mere idle and impertinent curiosity," he postulated, "is one thing: honest neighbourly interest is another. If I were a bolder man, I should ask you point-blank what part of Italy your part of Italy is."

Susanna (all a soft whiteness, in her white frock, in the mellow penumbra of the pine-grove) leaned back, and softly laughed.

"My part of Italy? That is not altogether easy to tell," she said, considering. "In one sense, my part of Italy is Rome. I belong to a Roman family, and am politically a subject of the Holy Father,—what though, for the moment, his throne be usurped by the Duke of Savoy, and his prerogatives exercised by the Camorra. But then my part of Italy is also Venice. We are Venetians, if to have had a house in Venice for some four hundred years is sufficient to constitute folk Venetians. But the part of Italy where I most often live, the part I like best, is a part you will never have heard of—a little castaway island in the Adriatic, about fifty miles north from Ancona: a little mountainous island, all fragrant of rosemary and basil, all grey with olive-trees,—all grey, save where the grey is broken by the green of vineyards, or the white and green of villas with their gardens, or the white and red of villages, with their red roofs, and white walls and campanili,—all grey, and yet all blue and gold, between the blue sea and the blue sky, in the golden light,—the little, unknown, beautiful island of Sampaolo."

She was actress enough to look unconscious and unconcerned, as she pronounced the name of Sampaolo. Her eyes gazed dreamily far away, as if they could behold an air-vision of her island. At the same time, I suspect, they kept a vigilant side-watch on Anthony.

Did Anthony give never so slightly perceptible a start? Did *his* eyes quicken? Did he colour a little? At all events, we need not question, he was aware of a sudden throb of excitement,—on the spur of which, without stopping to reflect, "Really?" he exclaimed. "That is a very odd coincidence. Sampaolo—I know all about it."

"Indeed?" said Susanna, looking surprise. "You have been there? It is rarely visited by travellers—except commercial ones."

"No, I have never been there," he answered, so far truthfully enough. "But—but I know—I used to know—a man whose—a man who had," he concluded lamely. For, when he did stop to reflect, "If you care for an amusing situation," he reflected, "you 'll leave her in the dark touching your personal connection with Sampaolo."

Susanna, being quite in the light touching that connection, could not help smiling.

"I must play the game on his conditions, and feign ignorance of all that he does n't tell," she reminded herself. "But fancy his being so secretive!"

"I hope the 'man who had' reported favourably of us?" she threw out.

"H'm—yes," said Anthony, with deliberation. "The truth is, he reported nothing. He was one of those inarticulate fellows who travel everywhere, and can give no better account of their travels than just a catalogue of names. He chanced to let fall that he had visited Sampaolo, and I thus learned that such a place existed. I can't tell why, but the fact struck me, and stuck in my mind, and I have ever since been curious to know something about it."

"You said you knew *all* about it," Susanna complained, her eyes rebukeful, her tone a tone of disappointment.

"Oh, that was a manner of speaking," Anthony quibbled, plausible and unperturbed. "I meant that I knew of its existence—which, after all, is relatively a good deal, being vastly more than most people know."

"It would be worth your while," said Susanna, "the next time you find yourself in its vicinity, to do Sampaolo the honour of an inspection. It is easily reached. The Austrian-Lloyd coasting steamers from Venice call there once a week, and there is a boat every Monday and Thursday from Ancona. Sampaolo is an extremely interesting spot,—interesting by reason of its natural beauty, its picturesque population, and (to me, at least) by reason of its absurdly romantic, serio-comic, lamentable little history."

"Ah—?" said Anthony, but with a suspension of the voice, with a solicitude of eye and posture, that pressed her to continue.

"He is a poor dissembler," thought Susanna. "As if any mere chance outsider would care a fig to hear about Sampaolo. However, so much the better."

"Yes," she said, and again she seemed rapt in dreamy contemplation of an air-vision. "The natural beauty of Sampaolo is to my thinking unparalleled. At a distance, as your ship approaches it, Sampaolo lies on the horizon like a beautiful soft cloud, all vague rose-colours and purples, a beautiful soft pinnacle of cloud. Then gradually, as you come nearer, the cloud changes, crystallises; and Sampaolo is like a great wonderful carving, a great wonderful carved jewel, a cameo cut on the sea, with a sort of aureole about it, an opalescence of haze and sunshine. Nearer still, its aspect is almost terrible, a scene of breath-taking precipices, spire-like mountains, wild black gorges, ravines; but, to humanise it, you can count at least twenty villages, villages clinging to every hillside, perched on almost every hill-top, each with its group of cypresses, like sentinels, and its campanile. At last you pass between two promontories, the Capo del Turco and the Capo del Papa, from the summits of which two great Crucifixes look down, and you enter the Laguna di Vallanza, a land-locked bay, tranquil as a lake. And there, floating on the water as it seems, there is a palace like a palace in Fairyland, a palace of white marble, all stately colonnades and terraces, yet looking, somehow, as light as if it were built of the sea's foam. This is one of the palaces—the summer palace—of the Counts of Sampaolo. It seems to float on the water, but it really occupies a tiny mite of an islet, called Isola Nobile; and connected with Isola Nobile by marble bridges are two other tiny Islets, laid out in gardens, Isola Fratello and Isola Sorella. The Counts of Sampaolo are one of the most ancient and illustrious families in Europe, the Valdeschi della Spina, descendants of San Guido Valdeschi, a famous soldier-saint of the Twelfth Century. They have another palace in the town of Vallanza, their winter palace, the Palazzo Rosso; and a splendid old mediaeval castle, Castel San Guido, on the hill behind the town; and two or three delightful villas in different parts of the island. A highly enviable family, are they not? Orange-trees are in blossom at Sampaolo the whole year round, in blossom and in fruit at the same time. The olive orchards of Sampaolo are just so many wildernesses of wild flowers: violets, anemones, narcissus; irises, white ones and purple ones; daffodils, which we call asphodels; hyacinths, tulips, arums, orchids—oh, but a perfect riot of wild flowers. In the spring the valleys of Sampaolo are pink with blossoming peach-trees and almond-trees, where they are not scarlet with pomegranates. Basil, rosemary, white heather, you can pluck where you will. And everywhere that they can find a footing, oleanders grow, the big double red ones, great trees of them, such wonder-worlds of colour, such fountains of perfume. The birds of Sampaolo never cease their singing— they sing as joyously in December as in June. And the nightingales of

Sampaolo sing all day, as well as all night. *Tiu, tiu, tiu—will, will, will—weep, weep, weep*—I can hear them now. But I must stop, or I shall go on for ever. Believe me, the beauties of Sampaolo are very great."

It was a long speech, but it had had an attentive listener. It was a long speech, but it had been diversified by the varying modulations of Susanna's voice, the varying expressions of her face, by little pauses, hesitations, changes of time and of rhythm, by occasional little gestures.

It had had an attentive, even an absorbed listener: one who, already interested in the speaker, happened to have a quite peculiar interest in her theme. As she spoke, I think Anthony beheld his own air-vision of Sampaolo; I fancy the familiar park of Craford, the smooth, well-groomed, well-fed English landscape, melted away; I doubt if he saw anything of the actual save the white form, the strenuous face, the shining eyes, of his informant.

But now, her voice ceasing, suddenly the actual came back—the brown brook swirling at their feet, the tall pines whispering above, the warm pine-incense, the tesserae of sun and shadow dancing together on the carpet of pine-needles, as the tassels overhead swung in the moving air.

"You paint Elysium," he said. "You paint a veritable Island of the Blessed."

Susanna's eyes clouded.

"Once upon a time Sampaolo *was* a veritable Island of the Blessed," she answered sadly. "But now no more. Since its union with what they call the Kingdom of Italy, Sampaolo has been, rather, an Island of the Distressed."

"Ah—?" said Anthony, again on a tone, with a mien, that pressed her to continue.

But all at once, as if recalled from an abstraction, Susanna gave a little laugh,—what seemed a slightly annoyed, half-apologetic little laugh,—and lifted her hands in a gesture of deprecation, of self-reprehension.

"I beg your pardon," she said. "I can't think how I have allowed myself to become so tiresome. One prates of one's parish pump."

"*Tiresome?*" cried out Anthony, in spontaneous protest. "I can't tell you how much you interest me."

"He is the poorest of poor dissemblers," thought Susanna.

"You are extremely civil," she said. "But how can the condition of our parish pump possibly interest a stranger?"

"H'm," thought Anthony, taken aback, "I expect my interest *does* seem somewhat improbable."

So, speciously, he sought to justify it.

"For more reasons than a few," he alleged. "To begin with, if I dared, I should say because it is *your* parish pump." He ventured a little bow. "But, in the next place, because it is an Italian parish pump, and somehow everything connected with Italy interests one. Then, because it is the parish pump of Sampaolo, and I have always been curious about Sampaolo. And finally, because it is a *human* parish pump—*et nihil humanum* . . . . So please go on. How did Sampaolo come to be an Island of the Distressed?"

"He 's not such a poor dissembler, after all,—when roused to action," thought Susanna. "But perhaps we have had enough Sampaolo for one session. I must leave him with an appetite for more."

"Hark," she said, raising a finger, while her face became intent. "Is n't that a skylark?"

Somewhere—just where one could n't tell at first—a bird was singing. Many birds were singing, innumerable birds were chirruping, all about. But this bird's song soared clear above the others, distinct from them, away from them, creating for itself a kind of airy isolation. It was an exquisitely sweet, liquid song, it was jocund, joyous, and it was sustained for an astonishing length of time. It went on and on and on, never faltering, never pausing, in soft trills and gay roulades, shrill skirls or flute-like warblings, a continuous outpour, for I don't know how many minutes. It was a song marvellously apposite to the bright day and the wide countryside. The freshness of the air, the raciness of the earth, the green of grass and trees, the laughing sunlight,—one might have fancied it was the spirits of all these singing together in unison.

"It's a skylark, sure enough," said Anthony, looking skywards. "But where the mischief is he?"

And they gave eyes and ears to trying to determine, searching the empyrean. Now his voice seemed to come from the west, now from the north, the south, the east; it was the most deceptive, the most elusive thing.

"Ah—there he is," Anthony cried, of a sudden, and pointed.

"Where? Where?" breathlessly asked Susanna, anxious as if life and death hung on the question.

"There—look!" said Anthony, pointing again.

High, high up in the air, directly over their heads, they could discern a tiny speck of black against the blue of the sky. They sat with their necks craned back as far as they would go, and gazed at it like people transfixed, whilst the sky pulsated to their dazzled sight.

"It is incredible," said Susanna. "A mere pin-point in that immensity, yet he fills it full with his hosannas."

But the pin-point grew bigger, the hosannas louder; the bird was descending.

"Literally it is music coming down upon us from heaven," she said.

"Yes—but when it reaches us, it will stop, we shall lose it," said Anthony. "It is music too ethereal to survive the contact of this gross planet."

Singing, singing, the bird sank, with folded wings; and sure enough, the very instant he touched the earth, his song stopped short—a bubble pricked, a light extinguished.

"He has come to drink and bathe," said Susanna.

He was hopping towards the water, on the other side of the brook, for a poet the most prosaic-looking fellow, in the soberest brown coat. Evidently he did n't dream that he was not alone. The trees had no doubt hidden his watchers. But now Susanna's voice startled him. With one wild glance at them, and a wild twitter of surprise, self-rebuke, consternation, he bounded into the air, and in a second was a mere speck again.

"Oh, how silly of him," Susanna sighed. "Does he think we are dragons?"

"No," said Anthony. "He would n't be half so frightened if he thought we were dragons. He thinks we are much worse."

"Oh—?" guilelessly questioned she. "What is that?"

"He thinks we are human beings," Anthony explained.

Susanna laughed, but it was rather a rueful laugh.

"Anyhow," she said, "he 'll not come back so long as we remain here. Yet he is hot and thirsty—and who knows from what a distance he may have flown, just for this disappointment? Don't you think it would be gracious on our part if we were to remove the cause of his alarm?"

She rose, and led the way out of the pine-grove, towards her house. When they reached the open, it was to discover, walking together from the opposite direction, Adrian and Miss Sandus,—Adrian bending towards his companion in voluble discourse, which he pointed and underlined by copious gesticulation.

"Enter Rumour, painted full of tongues," Anthony murmured, more or less in his sleeve.

But at sight of him, Adrian halted, and struck an attitude.

"Oh, the underhand, the surreptitious villain!" he cried out. Then he turned his pink face towards Susanna. "Lady, beauteous lady, vision of loveliness," he saluted her, bowing to the ground. "But oh, to think of that dark, secret villain! He 's gone and made your acquaintance without waiting for me to introduce him, which I was so counting upon doing to-morrow morning. Already he groans and totters under the weight of obligations I 've heaped upon him. I wanted to add one more—and now he 's gone and circumvented me."

"You will add one more if you 'll be so good as to introduce me to Miss Sandus," said Anthony.

And when the introduction was accomplished, he proceeded to make himself as agreeable to that lady as he possibly could. In the first place, he liked her appearance, he liked her brisk, frank manner; and then, is n't it always well to have a friend near the rose?

The result was that when she and Susanna were alone, Miss Sandus succinctly remarked, "My dear, your cousin is a trump."

X

The shadows were long, as he and Adrian strolled back to Craford Old Manor.

"Well, now, Truepenny," Adrian began, "now that you 've met her, speak out, and tell me on your heart and conscience how she impresses you."

"She seems all right," was Anthony's temperate reply.

"*All right?*" cried Adrian, looking scorn and pity. "My dear Malaprop, she 's just simply the nicest person of her sex within the confines of the Solar System. She is to other women what—well, I 'll name no names—what somebody I *could* name is to other men. And with such eyes—hey? Are they bright? Are they sharp? Are they trusty? Are they knowing?"

"I expect she can see with them," said Anthony.

"*See* with them," Adrian sniffed. "I 'll tell you what she can do—she can see round a corner with them. And then such pretty little ears, besides. Did you notice her ears?"

"I noticed she was n't earless," Anthony admitted.

"*Earless*," cried Adrian. "Her ears are like roses and white lilies. Earless, says he. I 'll bet three-halfpence you 'll presently be denying that she 's witty."

"She seems witty enough," assented Anthony.

"*Witty*," Adrian scoffed, cutting a caper to signify his disdain for the weak expression. "Witty is n't the word for it. And then, with all her years, she 's so *young*, is n't she? She breathes the fresh, refreshing savour of an unspoiled soul."

"Yes, she's young—for the time being," Anthony agreed. "By the bye, do you know where she comes from?"

"*Do* I know? I should rather think I know," said Adrian, swaggering. "She has n't a secret from me. She comes from Westmoreland. They 're an old Westmoreland family. But she lives in Kensington. She has one of those jolly old houses in Kensington Square. Historic, romantic, poetic Kensington Square, where burning Sappho loved and sang, and Thackeray wrote the What-do-you-call-'ems. Who fears to speak of Ninety-eight? That's her number. Ninety-eight, Kensington Square, W. And whenever I have occasion to run up to town, mind, I 'm not to think of going to an hotel, I 'm to drive straight to Ninety-eight, and it will be her joy to take me in. So it sometimes pays to be charming, after all."

"I see," said Anthony.

"You see? The deuce you do. What do you see?" asked Adrian, opening his blue eyes wide, and peering about, as one who would fain see too.

"You patter of Miss Sandus," said Anthony.

Adrian came to a standstill, and raised his hands towards heaven.

"Now I call upon the choirs of blessed Cherubim and Seraphim," he exclaimed. "I call upon them to suspend their singing for an instant, and to witness this. He sees that I patter of Miss Sandus. What perspicuity. And he just a mortal man, like anybody—nay, by all accounts, just a bluff country squire. Ah, what a noble understanding. Well, then, my dear Hawkshaw, since there's no concealing anything from you,—*fine mouche, allez!*—I own up. I patter of Miss Sandus."

"Do you happen to know where Madame Torrebianca comes from?" Anthony asked.

"Oho!" cried Adrian. "It's Madame Torrebianca that *you 've* been raving about. Ah, yes. Oh, I concede at once that Madame Torrebianca is very nice too. None readier than I to do her homage. But for fun and devilment give me Peebles. Give me old ladies, or give me little girls. You 're welcome to the betwixts and the betweens. Old ladies, who have passed the age of folly, or little girls, who have n't reached it. But women in the prime of their womanhood are always thinking of fashion-plates and curling-irons and love and shopping. Name me, if you can, four vainer, tiresomer, or more unfruitful topics. Have you never waked in your bed at midnight to wonder how it has come to pass that I, at my time of life, with my attractions, am still a bachelor? To wonder what untold disappointment, what unwritten history of sorrow, has left me the lonely, brooding celibate you see? I 'll lift the veil—a moment of épanchement. It's because I 've never met a marriageable woman who had n't her noddle stuffed with curling-irons and fashion-plates and love and shopping."

"Do you happen to know where she comes from?" Anthony repeated.

"She—? Who?" asked Adrian, looking vague. Then, as Anthony vouchsafed no answer, but merely twirled his stick, and gazed with indifferent eyes at the horizon, "Oh—Madame Torrebianca?" he conjectured. "Still harping on my daughter? Of course I know where *she* comes from. She comes from the land where the love of the turtle now melts into sweetness, now maddens to crime—as who should say a land of

Guildhall banquets. She comes from Italy. Have you ever eaten ortolans in Italy?"

"Do you happen to know what part of Italy?" Anthony persisted.

"From Rome, the pomp and pageant of imperial Rome," returned Adrian promptly. "I 've got it in the lease. Nothing like having things in leases. The business instinct—what? Put it in black and white, says I. 'La Nobil Donna Susanna Torrebianca, of the Palazzo Sebastiani, via Quattro Fontane, Rome, party of the second part.' A *beau vers*, is n't it? The lilt, the swelling cadence, the rich rhyme, the hidden alliterations,—and then the sensitive, haunting pathos, the eternal verities adumbrated by its symbolism. I 've stood upon Achilles' tomb, and heard Troy doubted. Time—that monster-mother, who brings forth her children only to devour them—Time shall doubt of . . ."

"Rome may be the official sort of address she gives to land-agents and people," Anthony interposed. "But the part of Italy where she really lives is a little castaway island in the Adriatic, some fifty miles north from Ancona,—the little, unknown, beautiful island of Sampaolo."

Adrian came to a standstill again, and dropped his jaw in sign of astonishment.

"Oh, come. Not really?" he gasped at length.

"Yes, really," said Anthony.

"My eye!" Adrian exclaimed.

"It *is* odd, is n't it?" said Anthony.

"*Odd?*" cried Adrian. "It's—it—it beggars the English tongue."

"Well, if it beggars yours, it is doing pretty well," said Anthony.

"You goose," said Adrian, resuming his walk. "Can you actually suppose that I 've passed all these golden days and weeks in friendly hob-nobbings with her, and not learned that she came from the island of Sampaolo? A fellow of penetration, like me? I appeal to your honour—is it likely?"

"Why the devil have you never told me?" Anthony demanded, with asperity.

"You 've never asked me—you 've never given me a chance. You talk, when you have me for a listener, you talk such an uninterrupted stream, it's a miracle if I ever get a word in edgewise," Adrian explained.

"I trust, at least, that you 've been equally taciturn with her," said Anthony.

"My good Absolute, I am the soul of taciturnity," Adrian boasted, expanding his chest, and thumping it. "This bosom is a sealed sanctuary for the confidences of those who confide in me. Besides, when I 'm with Madame Torrebianca, believe me, we have other subjects of conversation than the poor Squire o' Craford."

"You see," said Anthony, "for the lark of the thing, I should like, for the present, to leave her in ignorance of my connection with Sampaolo."

"That's right," cried Adrian. "Dupe, cozen, jockey the trustful young creature. Do. There 's a great-hearted gentleman. You need n't fear *my* undeceiving her. I know my place; I know who holds the purse-strings; I know which side my bread is buttered on. Motley's my wear. So long as you pay my wages, you may count upon my connivance."

"I shall see her to-morrow morning at Mass. I wonder whether I am in love with her," Anthony was thinking.

XI

He gave her holy water at the door of the chapel, and her eyes acknowledged it with a glance that sent something very pleasant into his heart.

Then, with an impulse of discretion, to efface himself, he knelt at the first prie-dieu he came to. But Susanna, instead of going forward, knelt at the prie-dieu next to his.

The chapel at Craford is a dim, brown little room,—the same room that in the days of persecution had been a "secret" chapel, where priests and people worshipped at the peril of their lives. You enter it from the hall by a door that was once a sliding panel. In the old days there was no window, but now there is a window, a small one, lancet-shaped, set with stained glass, opening into the court. Save for the coloured light that came through this, and the two candles burning on the altar, the chapel was quite dark. The Mass was said by an old Capuchin, Father David, from the convent at Wetherleigh; it was served by Adrian.

You know "the hidden and unutterable sweetness of the Mass."

For Anthony, kneeling there with Susanna, the sweetness of the Mass was strangely intensified. He did not look at her, he looked at the altar, or sometimes at his prayer-book; but the sense that she was beside him possessed every atom of his consciousness. Her kneeling figure, her white profile, her hair, her hat, her very frock,—he could see them, somehow, without looking; his eye preserved a permanent vision of them. Yet they did not distract his thoughts from the altar. He followed with devout attention the Act that was being consummated there; the emotion of her presence merged with and became part of the emotion of the Mass. They were offering the Holy Sacrifice side by side, they were offering it together, they were sharing the Sacred Mystery. It seemed to him that by this they were drawn close to each other, and placed in a new relation, a relation that was far beyond the mere acquaintanceship of yesterday, that in a very special and beautiful way was intimate. The priest crossed the sanctuary, and they stood together for the Gospel; the bell was rung, and together they bowed their heads for the Elevation. They knelt side by side in body, but in spirit was it not more than this? In spirit, for the time, were they not absolutely at one?—united, commingled, in the awe and the wonder, the worship and the love, of the Presence that had come, that was filling the dim and silent little chapel with a light eyes were not needed to see, with a music ears were not needed to hear, that had transformed the poor little altar into a painless

Calvary, whence were diffused all peace, all grace, all benediction? They knelt side by side, adoring together, breathing together the air that was now in very deed the air of Heaven. And it seemed to Anthony as if the Presence smiled upon them, and sanctioned and sanctified the thing that was in his heart.

"Domine, non sum dignus," solemnly rose the voice of the priest, "Domine, non sum dignus . . ."

It was the supreme moment.

They went forward, and side by side knelt at the rail of the sanctuary.

XII

Alas, the uncertain glory of an English June. That night the weather changed. Monday was grey and cold, the beginning of a cold grey week, a week of rain and wind, of low skies and scudding clouds; the sad-coloured sea flecked with angry white, the earth sodden; leaves, torn from their trees, scurrying down the pathways; and Adrian, of all persons, given over to peevishness and lamentations.

"Oh, I brazenly confess it—I 'm a fair-weather friend," he said, as he looked disconsolately forth from the window of his business-room, (a room, by the bye, whereof the chief article of furniture was a piano-à-queue). "Bring me sunshine and peaches, and I 'll be as sweet as bright Apollo's lute strung with his hair. But this sort of gashly, growsy, grim, sour, shuddery weather turns me into a broken-hearted vixen. I could sit down and cry. I could lie down and die. I could rise up and snap your head off. I am filled with verjuice and vitriol. Oh, me! Oh, my!"

He stamped backwards and forwards, in nervous exasperation. He went to the piano, and brought his hands down in a discordant clang upon the keys.

"Can't anybody silence those stupid *birds*?" he cried, moving back to the window, through which the merry piping of a robin was audible. "How inept, how spiteful, of them to go on singing, singing, in the face of such odious weather. Tell Wickersmith or someone to take a gun and an umbrella, and to go out and shoot them. And the wind—the strumpet wind," he cried. "All last night it gurgled and howled and hooted in my chimney like a drunken banshee, and nearly frightened me to death. And me a musician. And me the gentlest of God's creatures—who never did any harm, but killed the mice in father's barn. I ask you, as a man of the world, is it delicate, is it fair? Drip, drip, drip—swish, swish, swash,—ugh, the rain! If it could *guess* how I despise it!" He made a face and shook his fist at it. "Do you think the weather *knows* how disagreeable it is? We all know how disagreeable other people can be, but so few of us know how disagreeable we ourselves can be. Do you think the weather knows? Do you think it's behaving in this way purposely to vex me?"

But for Anthony it was a period not without compensations. He saw Susanna nearly every day. On Tuesday she and Miss Sandus were his guests at dinner; on Wednesday he and Adrian were her guests at luncheon; on Thursday, at tea-time, they paid their visit of digestion; on Friday, the rain holding up for a few hours in the afternoon, he and Susanna went for a walk on the cliffs.

The sea-wind buffetted their faces, it lifted Susanna's hair and blew stray locks about her temples, it summoned a lively colour to her cheeks. Anthony could admire the resolute lines, the forceful action, of her strong young body, as she braced herself to march against it. From the turf under their feet rose the keen odour of wet earth, and the mingled scents of clover and wild thyme. All round them sand-martins wheeled and swerved, in a flight that was like aerial skating. Far below, and beyond the dark-green of Rowland Marshes, which followed the winding of the cliffs like a shadow, stretched the grey sea, with its legions of white horses.

"What a sense one gets, from here, of the sea's immensity," Susanna said. "I think the horizon is a million miles away."

"It is," affirmed Anthony, with conclusiveness, as one possessing exact knowledge. Then, in a minute, "And, as we are speaking in round numbers, are you aware that it's a million years since I last had the pleasure of a word with you?"

Susanna's dark eyes grew big.

"A million years? Is it really," she doubted, in astonishment.

"Really and truly," asseverated he.

"A million years! How strange," she murmured, as one in a maze.

"Truth is often strange," said he.

"Yes—but this is particularly strange," she pointed out. "Because, first, we have only known each other a week. And, secondly, I was under the impression that you had had 'a word with me' yesterday—and again the day before yesterday—and again the day before that."

"I beg your pardon," said he. "I have not had a word with you since we sat by the brink of your artificial streamlet last Saturday afternoon; and that, speaking in round numbers, was a million years ago. As for yesterday, and the day before yesterday, and the day before that,—I don't count it having a word with you when we are surrounded by strangers."

"Strangers—?" wondered Susanna.

"Yes," said he. "That fellow Willes, and your enchanting friend Miss Sandus."

Susanna gave one of her light trills of laughter.

"We can't discuss our private affairs before them," said Anthony; "and I 've been pining to discuss our private affairs."

"Have we private affairs?" Susanna questioned, in surprise.

"Of course we have," said he. "Everybody has. And it is to discuss them that I have inveigled you into taking this walk with me. Does n't the sort of English weather you 're at present getting a taste of make you wish you had never left Italy?"

"Oh," she acquainted him, "it sometimes rains in Italy."

"Does it, indeed?" he enquired, opening his eyes. "But never—surely never—at Sampaolo?"

"Yes, even sometimes at Sampaolo," she laughed. "And mercy, how the wind can blow there! This is nothing to it. I don't think you have any winds in England so violent as our *temporali*."

Anthony nodded, with satisfaction.

"Please go on," he urged. "I have been longing to hear more about Sampaolo."

"Oh?" said Susanna, looking sceptical. "I feared I had wearied you inexcusably with Sampaolo."

"Every syllable you pronounced," vowed he, "was of palpitating interest, and you broke off at the most palpitating moment. You were on the point of telling me how, from an Island of the Blessed, Sampaolo came to be an Island of the Distressed—when we were interrupted by a skylark."

"That would be a terribly long story," Susanna premonished him, shaking her head.

"I adore terribly long stories," he declared. "And have we not before us the whole of future time?"

"Sampaolo came to be an Island of the Distressed," said she, "because, some half-century ago, the Sampaolesi got infected with an idea that was then a kind of epidemic—the idea of Italian unity. So they had a revolution, overthrew their legitimate sovereign, gave up their Independence, and united themselves to the 'unholy and unhappy State' which has since assumed the name of the Kingdom of Italy."

"That is not a terribly long story," Anthony complained. "I 'm afraid you are suppressing some of the details."

"Yes," she at once acknowledged, "I daresay I 'm suppressing a good many of the details."

"That's not ingenuous," said he, "nor—nor kind."

"It was not unkindly meant," said she.

"But Sampaolo," he questioned, "had, then, been independent? Go on. Be communicative, be copious; tell me all about it."

"For more than seven hundred years," answered Susanna, "Sampaolo had been independent. The Counts of Sampaolo were counts regnant, holding the island by feudal tenure from the Pope, who was their suzerain, and to whom they paid a tribute. They were counts regnant and lords paramount, *tiranni*, as they were called in mediaeval Italy; they had their own coinage, their own flag, their own little army; and though some of the noble Sampaolese families bore the title of prince or duke at Rome, they ranked only as barons at Sampaolo, and were subjects of the Count."

A certain enthusiasm rang in her voice. They walked on for some paces in silence.

"In the Palazzo Rosso at Vallanza, to this day," she continued, "you will be shown the throne-room, with the great scarlet throne, and the gilded coronet topping the canopy above it. But the Counts of Sampaolo were good men and wise rulers; and, under them, for more than seven hundred years, the island was free, prosperous, and happy. And though many times the Turks tried to take it, and many times the Venetians, and though sometimes the Pope tried to take it back, when the Pope happened to be a difficult Pope, the Sampaolesi, who were splendid fighters, always managed to hold their own."

Again they took some paces in silence.

"Then"—her voice had modulated—"then the idea of Italian unity was preached to them, and in 1850 they had a revolution; and foolish, foolish Sampaolo voluntarily submitted itself to the reign of Victor Emmanuel. And ever since,"—her eyes darkened,—"what with the impossible taxes, the military conscription, the corrupt officials, the Camorra, Sampaolo has been in a very wretched plight indeed. But—*pazienza*!" She gave her shoulders a light little shrug. "The Kingdom of Italy will not last forever."

"We will devoutly hope not," concurred Anthony. "Meanwhile, I am glad to note that in politics you are a true-blue reactionary."

"In Sampaolese politics," said she, "reaction would be progress. Before 1850 the people of Sampaolo were prosperous, now they are miserably poor; were pious, now they are horribly irreligious; were governed by honest gentlemen, now they form part of a nation that is governed by its criminal classes."

"And what became of the honest gentlemen?" Anthony enquired. "What did the counts do, after they were—'hurled,' I believe, is the consecrated expression—after they were hurled from their scarlet thrones?"

"Ah," said Susanna, seriously, "there you bring me to the chapter of the story that is shameful."

"Oh—?" said he, looking up.

"The revolution at Sampaolo was headed by the Count's near kinsman," she said. "The present legitimate Count of Sampaolo is an exile. His title and properties are held by a cousin, who has no more right to them, no more shadow of a right, of a moral right, than—than I have."

"Ah," said Anthony. And then, philosophically, "A very pretty miniature of an historical situation," he commented. "Orleans and Bourbon, Hanover and Stuart. A count in possession, and a count over the water, an usurper and a pretender."

"Exactly," she assented, "save that the Count in possession happens to be a Countess—the grand-daughter of the original usurper, whose male line is extinct. Oh, the history of Sampaolo has been highly coloured. A writer in some English magazine once described it as a patchwork of melodrama and opera-bouffe. It ended, if you like, in melodrama and opera-bouffe, but it began in pure romance and chivalry."

"Don't stop," said Anthony. "Tell me about the beginning."

"I can tell you that," announced Susanna, smiling, "in the words of your own English historian, Alban Butler."

She paused for an instant, as if to make sure of her memory, and then, smiling, recited—

"'In the year 1102 or 1103,' he says, in his Life of St. Guy Valdescus of The Thorn, as he Anglicises San Guido Valdeschi della Spina, 'when the Saint was returning from the Holy Land, where he had been a crusader, he was shipwrecked, by the Providence of God, upon the island of Ilaria, in the Adriatic Sea; and he was greatly afflicted by the discovery that the inhabitants of that country were almost totally ignorant of the truths of our Holy Religion, while the little knowledge they possessed was confused with many diabolical superstitions. They still invoked the daemons of pagan mythology, and sacrilegiously included our Divine Lord and His Blessed Mother in the number of these. Now, St. Guy had distinguished himself in the Crusade alike for his valour in action, for the edifying character of his conversation, and for the devotion and recollection with which he performed the exercises of religion; and he was surnamed Guy of the Thorn for that he had caused to be fixed in the hilt of his sword a sharp thorn, or spine, which, when he fought, should prick the flesh of his hand, and thus keep him in mind of the pious purpose for which he was fighting, and that it behoved a soldier of the Cross to fight, not in private anger or martial pride, but in Christian zeal and humility. When, therefore, after his shipwreck, and after many other perils and adventures by sea and land, the Saint finally arrived at Rome, of which city his family were patricians, and where his venerable mother, as well as his wife and children, eagerly awaited his return, he was received with every sign of favour by the Pope, Pascal the Second, who commended him warmly upon the good reports he had had of him, and asked him to choose his own reward. St. Guy answered that for his reward he prayed he might be sent back to the island of Ilaria, with a bishop and a sufficient company of priests, there to spread the pure light of the Faith among the unfortunate natives. Whereupon the Pope created him Count and Governor of the country, the heathen name of which he changed to St. Paul, and gave him as the emblem of his authority a sword in the hilt of which was fixed a thorn of gold. This holy relic, under the name of the Spina d'Oro, is preserved, for the reverence of the faithful. In the cathedral of the city of Vallanza, where the descendants of St. Guy still reign as lieutenants of the Sovereign Pontiff.'—There," concluded Susanna, with a little laugh, "that is the Reverend Alban Butler's account of the matter."

"I stand dumb with admiration," professed Anthony, his upcast hand speaking volumes, "before your powers of memory. Fancy being able to quote Alban Butler word for word, like that!"

"When I was young," Susanna explained, "I was made by my English governess to learn many of Butler's Lives by heart, and, as an Ilarian, the Life of San Guido interested me particularly. He was canonised, by the way, by Adrian the Fourth—the English Pope. As a consequence of that, the Valdeschi have always had a great fondness for England, and have often married English wives—English Catholics, of course. An Englishwoman was Countess of Sampaolo when the end came, the patchwork end."

"Ah, yes," said Anthony, "the patchwork end—tell me about that."

"The end," Susanna answered, "was an act of shameful treachery on the part of one of the descendants of San Guido towards another, his immediate kinsman, and the rightful head of the family. And now it is melodrama and opera-bouffe as much as ever you will. It is a revolution in a tea-cup. It is the ancient story of the Wicked Uncle."

"Yes?" said Anthony.

"It is perfectly trite," said Susanna, "and it would be perfectly absurd, if it were n't rather tragic, or perfectly tragic, if it were n't rather absurd."

She thought for a moment. Anthony waited, attentive.

"In 1850," she narrated, "Count Antonio the Seventeenth died, leaving a widow, who was English, and an only son, a lad of twelve, who should naturally have succeeded his father as Guido the Eleventh. But Count Antonio had a younger brother, also named Guido, who coveted the succession for himself, and had long been intriguing to secure it— organising secret societies among the people, to further the idea of Italian unity, and bargaining with the King of Sardinia for the price he should receive if he contrived to bring the Sampaolesi to give up their independence. Well," she went on, with a slight effect of effort, "while his brother lay dying, Guido, spying his opportunity, was especially active. 'Now,' he said to the people, 'is the time to strike. If, at my brother's death, his son succeeds him, we shall have a regency, and the regent will be a foreigner and a woman. Now is the time to terminate this petty despotism forever, to repudiate the suzerainty of the Pope, and to join in the great movement of Italia Riunita. To the Palace! Let us seize the Englishwoman and her son, and banish them from the island. Let us hoist the tricolour, and proclaim ourselves Italians, and subjects of the King. To the Palace!' So, while that poor lady"—her voice quavered a little—"while that poor lady was kneeling at the bedside of her dead husband,"—her voice sank,— "a great mob of insurgents broke into the Palazzo Rosso, singing 'Fuori l'Italia lo straniero,' seized her and the little Count, dragged them to the sea-front, and put them aboard a ship that was leaving for Trieste."

She paused for a few seconds.

"Then there was a plebiscite," she proceeded, "and Sampaolo solemnly transformed itself into a province of the Kingdom of Sardinia."

She paused again.

"And the Wicked Uncle," she again proceeded, "received his price from Turin. First, he was appointed Prefect of Sampaolo for life. Secondly, the little Count and his mother were summoned to take the oath of fidelity to the King, and as they did not turn up to do so, having gone to her people in England, they were declared to have outlawed themselves, and to be 'civilly dead', their properties, accordingly, passing to the next heir, who, of course, was Guido himself. Thirdly, Guido was created Count of Sampaolo by royal patent, the Papal dignity being pronounced 'null and not recognisable in the territories of the King.' It is Guido's granddaughter who is Countess of Sampaolo to-day."

She terminated her narration with a motion of the hand, as if she were tossing something from her. Anthony waited a little before he spoke.

"And the little Count?" he said, at length.

"The little Count," said Susanna, "went through the formality of suing his uncle for the recovery of his estates—or, rather, his mother, as his guardian, did so for him. But as the action had to be tried in the law-courts at Turin, I need n't tell you how it ended. In fact, it was never tried at all. For at the outset the judges decided that the suitor would have no standing before them until he had taken the oath of allegiance to the King, and renounced his allegiance to the Pope. He was 'civilly dead'—he must civilly resuscitate himself. As he refused to do this, his cause was dismissed, unheard."

"And then—?" said Anthony.

"Then the little Count returned to England, and grew to be a big count, and married an Englishwoman, and had a son, and died. He was adopted by his mother's brother, an English country gentleman, who, surviving him, and being a bachelor, adopted his son in turn. The son, however, dropped his title of Count, a title more than seven hundred years old, and assumed the name of his benevolent great-uncle. I 'm not sure," she reflected, "that I quite approve of his dropping that magnificent old title."

"Oh, he very likely found it an encumbrance, living in England, as an Englishman—especially if he was n't very rich," said Anthony. "He very likely felt that it rendered him rather uncomfortably conspicuous. Besides, a man does n't actually *drop* a title—he merely puts it in his pocket—he can always take it out again. You don't, I suppose," he asked, with a skilfully-wrought semblance of indifference, "happen to remember the name that he assumed?"

"Of course, I happen to remember it," replied Susanna. "As you must perceive, the history of Sampaolo is a matter I have studied somewhat profoundly. How could I forget so salient a fact as that? The name that he assumed," she said, her air elaborately detached, "was Craford."

But Anthony evinced not the slightest sign of a sensation.

"Craford?" he repeated. "Ah, indeed? That is a good name, a good old south-country Saxon name."

"Yes," agreed Susanna; "but it is not so good as Antonio Francesco Guido Maria Valdeschi della Spina, Conte di Sampaolo."

"It is not so long, at any rate," said he.

"Nor so full of colour," supplemented she.

"As I hinted before, a name like a herald's tabard might be something of an inconvenience in work-a-day England," he returned. Then he smiled, rather sorrily. "So you 've known all there was to be known from the beginning, and my laborious dissimulation has been useless?"

"Not useless," she consoled him, her eyes mirthfully meeting his. "It has amused me hugely."

"You've—if you don't mind the expression—you've jolly well taken me in," he owned, with a laconic laugh.

"Yes," laughed she, her chin in the air.

And for a few minutes they walked on without speaking.

The wind buffetted their faces, it wafted stray locks of hair about Susanna's temples, it smelt of the sea and the rain-clouds, though it could not blow away the nearer, friendlier smell of the wet earth, nor the sweetness of the clover and wild thyme. All round them, sand-martins performed their circling, swooping evolutions. In great squares fenced by hurdles, flocks of sheep nibbled the wet grass. Far beneath, the waters stretched grey to the blurred horizon, where they and the low grey sky seemed one.

But I think our young man and woman were oblivious of things external, absorbed in their private meditations and emotions. They walked on without speaking, till a turn in the cliff-line brought them in sight of the little town of Blye, at the cliffs' base, where it rose from the surrounding green of Rowland Marshes like a smoky red island.

"Blye," said Anthony, glancing down.

"Yes," said Susanna. "I had no idea we had come so far."

"I 'm afraid we have come *too* far. I 'm afraid I have allowed you to tire yourself," said he, with anxiety.

"Tired!" she protested. "Could one ever get tired walking in such exhilarating air as this?"

And, indeed, her colour, her bright eyes, her animated carriage, put to scorn his apprehension.

"But we must turn back, all the same," she added, "or—we shall not be home for tea."

She spoke in bated accents, and made a grave face, as if to miss tea were to miss a function sacrosanct.

Anthony laughed, and they turned back.

"It's a bit of a coincidence," he remarked presently, "that, coming from Sampaolo, you should just have chanced to take a house at Craford."

"Nothing could be simpler," said Susanna. "I wished to pass the summer in England, and was looking for a country house. The agent in London mentioned Craford New Manor, among a number of others, and Miss Sandus and I came down to see it. The prospect of finding myself the tenant of my exiled sovereign rather appealed to me—appealed to my sense of romance and to my sense of humour. And then,"—her eyes brightened,—"when we met your perfectly irresistible Mr. Willes, hesitation was impossible. He kept breaking out with little snatches of song, while he was showing us over the place; and afterwards he invited us to his music-room, (or I think he called it his *business*-room), and sang properly to us—his own compositions. He even permitted me to play some of his accompaniments."

Anthony chuckled.

"I 'm sure he did—I see my Adrian," he said. "Well, I owe him more than he 's aware of."

"Your Excellency is the legitimate Count of Sampaolo," said Susanna. "Antonio, by the Grace of God, and the favour of the Holy See, Count of Sampaolo—thirty-fourth count, and eighteenth of the name. I am your very loyal subject. Let's conspire together for your restoration."

"You told me the other day that you were a subject of the Pope," Anthony objected.

"That is during this interregnum," she explained. "The Pope is our liege lord's liege lord, and, in our liege lord's absence, our homage reverts to him. I will never, at all events, admit myself to be a subject of the Duke of Savoy. Let's plot for your restoration."

"My 'restoration,' if that is n't too sounding a term, is a thing past praying for," said Anthony. "But I don't know that I should very keenly desire it, even if it were n't."

"What!" cried she. "Would n't it be fun to potentate it on a scarlet throne?"

"Not such good fun, I fancy, as it is to squire it in these green meadows," he responded. "Are n't scarlet thrones apt to be upholstered with worries and responsibilities?"

"Are n't green meadows sown thick with worries and responsibilities?" asked Susanna.

"Very likely," he consented. "But for a moderate stipend I can always hire a man like Willes to reap and deal with them for me."

"Could n't you hire 'a man like Willis' to extract them from your scarlet cushions? Potentates have grand viziers. Mr. Willes would make a delicious grand vizier," she reflected, with a kind of wistfulness.

"He would indeed," said Anthony. "And we should have comic opera again with interest."

"But you only look at it from a selfish point of view," said Susanna. "Think of poor Sampaolo—under the old régime, an Island of the Blessed."

"Seriously, is there at Sampaolo, the faintest sentiment in favour of a return to the old régime?" he asked.

"Seriously, and more 's the pity, not the faintest," Susanna confessed. "I believe I am the only legitimist in the island—save a few priests and nuns, and they don't count. I am the entire legitimist party."

She turned towards him, making a little bow.

"Yet there is every manner of discontent with the present régime," she said. "The taxes, the conscription, the difficulties put in the way of commerce, the monstrous number of officials, and the corruption of them one and all, are felt and hated by everyone. Under the old régime, for example," she illustrated, "Vallanza was a free port,—now we have to pay both a national duty and a municipal duty on exports as well as imports; nothing was taxed but land, and that very lightly—now nearly everything is taxed, even salt, even a working-man's tools, even a peasant's necessary donkey, so that out of every lira earned the government takes from forty to sixty centimes; the fisheries of Sampaolo, which are very valuable, were reserved for the Sampaolesi,—now they are open to all Italy, and Sampaolo, an island, cannot compete with Ancona, on the railway. In Sampaolo to-day, if you have any public business to transact, from taking out a dog license to seeking justice in the law-courts, every official you have to deal with, including the judges, expects his buonamano. If you post a letter, it is an even chance whether the Post-Office young men won't destroy the letter and steal the stamps; while, if you go to the Post-Office to buy stamps, it is highly possible that they will playfully sell you forged ones."

She gave a bitter little laugh.

"The present Prefect of Sampaolo," she continued her illustrations, "formerly kept a disreputable public house, a sailors' tavern, at Ancona. He is known to be a Camorrista; and though his salary is only a few thousand lire, he lives with the ostentation of a parvenu millionaire, and no one doubts where he gets his money. These evils are felt by everyone. But the worst evil of all is the condition of the Church. In the old days the

Sampaolesi were noted for their piety; now, even in modern irreligious Italy, you would seek far to unearth a people so flagrantly irreligious. From high to low the men are atheists; and the few men who are not, have to be very careful how they show it. It is as much as a tradesman's trade is worth, as much as an employé's place is worth, to go to Mass; the one will sit behind a deserted counter, the other will learn that his services are no longer needed. The present régime is liked by no one save the officials who benefit by it; but it tickles the vanity of the Sampaolesi to call themselves citizens of a Great Power; and so, though many are republicans, many socialists, none are legitimists. They would prefer any burden to the burden of insignificance; and under the reign of the Valdeschi, though free, prosperous, and happy, Sampaolo was insignificant."

"You paint a very sad state of things," said Anthony.

"Believe me," said Susanna, "my painting is pale beside the reality."

"And, apparently, a hopeless state," he added.

"Some day the Kingdom of Italy must end in a tremendous smash-up. Afterwards, perhaps, there will be a readjustment. Our hope is in that," said she.

"Meanwhile, you make it clear, I am afraid," he argued, "that we should gain only our labour for our pains in plotting a restoration."

"We should have the excitement of plotting," laughingly argued she.

"A plotter's best reward, like an artist's, you suggest, is the pleasure he takes in his work. But now you are inciting me to look at it again from the selfish point of view, for which a moment ago you were upbraiding me," he reminded her.

"*Do* look at it from the selfish point of view," inconsistent and unashamed, she urged. "Think of your lands, your houses, your palaces and gardens, Castel San Guido, Isola Nobile, think of your pictures, your jewels, the thousand precious heirlooms that are rightly yours, think of your mere crude money. How can you bear the thought that these are in the possession of a stranger—these, your inheritance, the inheritance of nearly eight hundred years? Oh, if I were in your place, the wrong of it would fill the universe for me. I could not endure it."

"One has no choice but to endure it," said he. "One benumbs resentment with a fatalistic 'needs must.'"

"One would do better to inflame resentment with a defiant 'where there 's a will there 's a way,'" Susanna answered.

"The way is not plain to see."

"No—but we must discover the way. That"—she smiled—"shall be the aim of our plotting."

And again for some time they walked on without speaking.

"If she could only guess how little my heart's desire is centred upon the lands and houses of Sampaolo," thought Anthony, "how entirely it is centred upon something much nearer home. I wonder what she would do if I should tell her."

And at that thought his heart winced with delight and terror.

He looked sidewise at her. Her dark hair curled about her temples, and drooped in a loose mass behind; her dark eyes shone; there was a warm colour in her cheeks. Her head held high, her body defined itself in lines of strength and beauty, as she walked by the cliff's edge, resisting the wind, with the sea and the sky for background. He looked at her, and wondered what would happen if he should tell her; and his heart glowed with delight, and winced with delight and terror,—glowed with delight in the supreme reality of her presence, winced with delight and terror at the imagination of telling her.

And then the suspended rain came down in a sudden pelting shower; and Anthony put up his umbrella. To keep in its shelter, they had to walk very close to each other, their arms touching sometimes. I daresay they were both pretty wet when they reached Craford New Manor, but I don't think either minded much.

Miss Sandus, who met them in the hall, insisted that Susanna must go upstairs and change; but to Anthony she said, "There 'll be tea in a minute or two," and led the way to the drawing-room, the big, oblong, sombre red-and-gold drawing-room, with its heavy furniture, its heavy red damask hangings, its heavy gilded woodwork, its heavy bronzes and paintings.

Wet as he was, he followed, and sat down, with his conductress, before the huge red-marble fireplace, in which a fire of logs was blazing—by no means unwelcome on this not-uncharacteristic English summer's day.

XIII

"Well, you 've had a good sousing—had you a good walk?" asked the little brisk old woman, in her pleasant light old voice.

"Yes—to Blye, or nearly," said Anthony. "The rain only caught us towards the end. But what I stand in need of now is your sympathy and counsel."

She sat back in a deep easy chair, her pretty little hands folded in her lap, her pretty little feet, in dainty slippers, high-heeled and silver-buckled, resting on a footstool. It was a pretty as well as a kind and clever face that smiled enquiringly up at him, from under her soft abundance of brown hair.

"What's the matter?" she asked.

"Nothing much. I 'm merely in love," he answered.

Miss Sandus sat forward.

"In love? That's delightful. Whom with? With me? Is this a declaration? Or a confidence?"

She fixed him with her humorous bright old eyes.

"It's both. Of course, I 'm in love with you. Everyone who knows you is that," he predicated. "But also," he added, on a key of profound melancholy, "if you will forgive my forcing the confidence upon you, also with *her*."

He glanced indicatively ceilingwards.

"H'm," Miss Sandus considered, looking into the fire, "also with *her*."

"Yes," said Anthony.

"H'm," repeated Miss Sandus. "You go a bit fast. How long have you known her?"

"All my life. I never lived until I knew her," he averred.

"It was inevitable that you should say that—men always say that," the lady generalised. "I heard it for the first time fifty-five years ago."

"Then, I expect, there must be some truth in it," was Anthony's deduction. "Anyhow, I have known her long enough. One does n't need *time* in these affairs. One recognises a perfect thing—one recognises one's affinity. One knows when one is hit. I 'm in love with her. Give me your sympathy and counsel."

"You have my sympathy. What counsel do you wish?"

"What shall I do?" asked Anthony. "Drown myself? Take to drink?"

"I should n't drown myself," said Miss Sandus. "Drowning is so wet and chilly; and I 'm told it's frightfully unbecoming, into the bargain. As for drink, I hear it's nothing like what it's cracked up to be."

"I daresay it is n't," admitted Anthony, with a sigh. "I suppose there's not the ghost of a chance for me?" he gloomed.

"H'm," said Miss Sandus.

"I suppose it would be madness on my part to speak to her?" he pursued.

"That would depend a good deal, I should think, on the nature of what you said," his counsellor suggested, smiling.

"If I said point-blank I loved her—?"

Miss Sandus looked hard at the fire, her brows drawn together, pondering. Her brows were drawn together, but the *vis comica* played about her lips.

"I think, if I were in your place, I should try it," she decided at last.

"*Would* you?" said Anthony, surprised, encouraged. But, in a second, despondency had closed round him again. "You see," he signified, "the situation is uncommonly delicate—one 's at a double and twisted disadvantage."

"How so?" Miss Sandus asked, looking up.

"She's established here for the summer. I, of all men, must n't be the one to make Craford impossible for her."

"I see," said Miss Sandus. "Yes, there's that to be thought of."

"There 's such a deuced lot of things to be thought of," said he, despairingly.

"Let's hear the deuced lot," said the lady, with business-like cheerfulness.

"Well, to begin with," he brought out painfully, "there 's the fact that she 's rich."

"Yes, she's rich," conceded Miss Sandus. "Does that diminish her attractions?"

"You know what I mean," groaned Anthony, with no heart for trifling.

"For the matter of that, are n't you rich yourself?" Miss Sandus retorted.

"Rich!" he cried. "I totter on the brink of destitution."

"Oh?" she murmured. "I 'd imagined you were by way of being rather an extensive land owner."

"So I am," said he. "And my rather extensive lands, what with shrinkages and mortgages, with wages, pensions, subscriptions, and general expenses,—I doubt if they yield a net income of fifteen hundred a year. And I 've not a stiver else in the world."

"Poor, poor young man," she laughingly commiserated him. "And yet I hardly think you 're poor enough to let the fact of her wealth weigh with you. If a man has enough for himself, it does n't matter how much more his wife may have, since he 'll not depend upon her for his support. I should n't lie awake o' nights, bothering about the money question."

Anthony got up, and stood at the end of the fireplace, with his elbow on the mantel.

"You 're awfully good," he said, looking down at the gracious little old figure in the easy chair.

"I 'm an old woman," said she. "All old women love a lover. You renew the romance of things for us. You transport us back, a century or so, to our hot youth, when George the Third was king, and we were lovers ourselves. *Et in Arcadia ego*—but I 've lost my Greek."

"You 'll never lose your Pierian," said Anthony, bowing.

He took her hand, bent over it, and touched it with his lips.

"If flattery can make friends, you 'll not lack 'em," said she, with a pretty, pleased old blush.

"But I 've not yet emptied my sack," said he, relapsing into gloom. "There's a further and perhaps a greater difficulty."

"Let's hear the further difficulty," cheerily proposed Miss Sandus. Then, as he appeared to hesitate, "Has it anything to do with her former marriage?"

"You divine my thoughts," he replied, in an outburst. "Yet," he more lightly added, "you know, I don't in the least believe in her former marriage. She seems so—well, if not exactly girlish, so young, so immaculately fresh, it's impossible to believe in. None the less, of course, it 's an irrevocable fact, and it's a complication. I must n't intrude on sacred ground. If she still grieves . . ."

A gesture conveyed the rest.

"Look here," said Miss Sandus, abruptly. "I'm going to betray a trust. Think what you will of me, I 'm going to violate a confidence. She does n't grieve, she has never grieved. Your intuitions about her are right to the letter. She was never married, except in name—it was purely a marriage of convenience—the man was a complete nonentity. Don't ask me the whys and the wherefores. But make what you will of that which I 've been indiscreet enough to tell you."

"I think you are an angel out of Heaven," cried Anthony, with ardour. "If you could know the load you have lifted from my heart, the balm you have poured into it."

"If you have n't wealth," Miss Sandus went on, summing the issue up, "you have a good position and—a *beau nom*. You have more than one indeed, if all I hear be true. You 're both of the old religion, you 're both at the mating age. In every way it would be a highly suitable match. Wait for a good occasion—occasion's everything. Wait for—what does the poet say?—for the time and the place and the loved one all together, and tell her that you love her. And now—here comes the tea."

And with the tea came Susanna, in a wonderful rustling blue-grey confection of the material that is known, I believe, as *voile*; and immediately after Susanna, Adrian.

XIV

Adrian was clearly in a state of excitement. His hair was ruffled, his pink face showed a deeper flush, his lips were parted, his bosom heaved.

He halted near the threshold, he threw up his hands, he rolled his eyes, he nodded. It was patent that something had happened.

"Oh, my dears! my dears!" he gasped.

His dears attended, curious, expectant. But as he stood silent, and merely cast intensely significant glances from one to the other, and thence to the walls and ceiling, Anthony, constituting himself spokesman for the company, asked, "Well—? What's the row?"

"Oh, my dears!" Adrian repeated, and advanced a few steps further into the room, his hands still raised.

"What *is* it?" besought Susanna, breathless.

"Oh, my dearie dears!" he gasped.

He sank upon a chair.

"I must have a cup of tea before I can speak. Perhaps a cup of tea will pull me together."

Susanna hastily poured and brought him a cup of tea.

"Ministering angel!" was his acknowledgment. He tasted his tea. "But oh—unkind—you 've forgotten the sugar." He gazed helplessly at the tea-table.

Anthony brought him the sugar-bowl.

"Are those cruffins?" he asked, eyeing a dish on the cake-stand.

"They 're mumpers," said Miss Sandus, pushing the cake-stand towards him. "But you 're keeping us on tenter-hooks."

"I 'm *so* sorry. It's beyond my control. I must eat a mumpet. Perhaps then I 'll be able to tell you all about it."

He ate his mumpet—with every sign of relish; he sipped his tea; his audience waited. In the end he breathed a deep, long sigh.

"I 've had an experience—I 've had the experience of my life," he said.

"Yes—?" said they.

"I could n't lose an instant—I had to run—to tell you of it. I felt it would consume me if I could n't share it."

Their faces proclaimed their eagerness to hear.

"May I have another cup?" he asked Susanna.

This time, however, he rose, and went to the table.

"The world is so strange," he said.

"Come! we 're waiting for the experience of your life," said Anthony.

"You must n't hurry me—you must n't worry me," Adrian remonstrated. "I 'm in a very over-wrought condition. You must let me approach it in my own way."

"I believe the flighty creature has forgotten it," said Anthony.

"Flighty creature?" Adrian levelled eyes black with reproach upon him. Then turning to the ladies: "That shows how he misunderstands me. Just because I had a witty mother,—just because I 'm not a stolid, phlegmatic ox of a John Bull,—just because I 'm sensitive and impressionable,—he calls me flighty. But you know better, *don't* you? You, with all your fine feminine instincts and perceptions, you know that I 'm really as steady and as serious as the pyramids of Egypt. Even my very jokes have a moral purpose—and what I teach in them, I learned in sorrow. Flighty!" He shot another black glance at the offender, and held out his cup for a third filling.

"Blessings be on the man who invented tea," he devoutly murmured. "On Friday especially"—he appealed to Susanna—"*is n't* it a boon? I don't know how one could get through Friday without it. You poor dear fortunate Protestants"—he directed his remark to Miss Sandus—"have no conception how frequently Friday comes. I think there are seven Fridays in the week."

Susanna was softly laughing, where (in that wonderful, crisp, fresh, close-fitting, blue-grey gown, with its frills and laces and embroideries) she sat in the corner of a long, red-damask-covered sofa, by the prettily decked tea-table. Anthony, standing near her, looking down at her, was conscious of a great content in his heart, and of a great craving. "How splendid she is. Was there ever such hair? Were there ever such eyes, such lips? Was there ever such a frock? And then that faint, faint, faintest perfume, like a remembrance of violets!" I daresay something to this effect was vaguely singing itself to his thoughts.

"But the experience of your life? The experience of your life?" Miss Sandus insisted.

"He's clean forgotten it," Anthony assured her.

"Forgotten it? Tush," Adrian flung back, with scorn. "But you 're all so precipitate. One has to collect one's faculties. There are fifty possible ways of telling a thing—one must select the most effective. And then, if you come to that, life has so many experiences, and so many different sorts of experience. Life, to the man with an open eye, is just one sequence of many-coloured astonishments. I never could and never shall understand how it is possible for people to be bored. What do you say "—he looked towards the piano—"to my singing you a little song?"

"You 're inimitable—but you 're inimitably exasperating." Miss Sandus gave him up, with a resigned toss of the head.

"Do sing us a little song," Susanna begged.

He set off, dancing, in the direction of the instrument. But midway there he stopped, and half turned round, poising, as it were, in his flight.

"Grave or gay? Sacred or profane?" he asked from over his shoulder.

"Anything—what you will," Susanna answered.

"I 'll sing you a little Ave Maria," he decided. Whereupon, instead of proceeding, he turned his back squarely upon the piano, and squarely faced his hearers.

"When a musician composes an Ave Maria," he instructed them, "what he ought to try for is exactly what those nice old Fifteenth Century painters in Italy tried for when they painted their Annunciations. He should try to represent what one would have heard, if one had been there, just as they tried to represent what one would have seen. Now, how was it? What would one have heard? What did our Blessed Lady herself hear? Look. It was the springtime, and it was the end of the day. And she sat in her garden. And God sent His Angel to announce the 'great thing' to her. But she must not be frightened. She, so dear to God, the little maid of fifteen, all wonder and shyness and innocence, she must not be frightened. She sat in her garden, among her lilies. Birds were singing round her; the breeze was whispering lightly in the palm-trees; near-by a brook was plashing; from the village came the rumour of many voices. All the pleasant, familiar sounds of nature and of life were in the air. She sat there, thinking her white thoughts, dreaming her holy day-dreams. And, half as if it were a day-dream, she saw an Angel come and kneel before her. But she was not frightened—for it was like a day-dream—and the Angel's face was so beautiful and so tender and so reverent, she could not have been frightened, even if it had seemed wholly real. He knelt before her, and his lips moved, but, as in a dream, silently. All the familiar music of the world went on—the bird-songs, the whisper of the wind, the babble of the brook, the rumour of the village. They all went on—there was no pause, no hush, no change—nothing to startle her—only, somehow, they seemed all to draw together, to become a single sound. All the sounds of earth and heaven, the homely, familiar sounds of earth, but the choiring of the stars too, all the sounds of the universe, at that moment, as the Angel knelt before her, drew together into a single sound. And 'Hail,' it said, 'hail Mary full of grace!'"

For a minute, after he had finished, Adrian stood still, and no one spoke. Then he returned to the fireside, and sank back into his chair.

"What a beautiful—what a divinely beautiful—idea," Susanna said at last, with feeling.

"Beautiful," emphatically chimed in Protestant Miss Sandus.

"Stand still, true poet that you are,—I know you, let me try and name you," laughed Anthony, from the hearth-rug.

"Chrysostom—he should be named Chrysostom," said Miss Sandus.

"The world is a garden of beautiful ideas," was Adrian's modest acceptance of these tributes. "One only has to cull them. But now"—he rose—"I must toddle home. Are you going my way?" he inquired of Anthony.

"What?" protested Miss Sandus. "You're leaving us, without telling the experience of your life—the experience that you 'had to run' to tell us!"

"And without singing us your song," protested Susanna.

Adrian wrung his hands.

"Oh, cruel ladies!" he complained. "How can you be so unjust? I have told you the experience of my life. And as for singing my song—"

"He can always leave off singing when he hears a master talk," put in Anthony.

"As for singing my song," said Adrian, ignoring him, "I must go home and try to write it."

XV

And then the weather changed again. The clouds drifted away, the sun came back, the sunshine was like gold that had been washed and polished. The landscape smiled with a new radiance, gay as if it had never gloomed. The grass was greener, the flowers were brighter, the birds sang louder and clearer. The sea, with its shimmer and sheen, was like blue silk; the sky was like blue velvet. The trees lifted up their arms, greedy for the returned light and warmth, the sweeter air.

Susanna, at noon-day, in her pine grove, by her brookside, was bending down, peering intently into the transparent water.

Anthony, seeking, found her there.

"Books in the running brooks. I interrupt your reading?" he suggested, as one ready, at a hint, to retire.

"No," said she, looking up—giving, for a second, her eyes to his, her dark, half-laughing eyes. "It is not a book—it is the genius of the place."

She pointed to where, at her feet, the hurrying stream rested an instant, to take breath, in a deep, dusky little pool, overhung by a tangle of eglantine.

"See how big he is, and how old and grey and grim, and how motionless and silent. It seems almost discourteous of him, almost contemptuous, not to show any perturbation when one intrudes upon him, does n't it?"

The genius of the place, floating in the still water, his fixed small beady eyes just above the surface, was a big grey frog.

"Books in the running brooks indeed, none the less," Susanna went on, meditating. "Brooks—even artificial ones—are so mysterious, are n't they? They are filled with so many mysterious living things—frogs and tadpoles and newts and strange water-insects, nixies and pixies. Undines and Sabrinas fair and water-babies; and such strange plants grow in them; and who can guess the meaning of the tales they tell, in that never-ceasing, purling tongue of theirs? . . . And Signor Ranocchio? What do you suppose he is thinking of, as he floats there, so still, so saturnine, so indifferent to us? He is plainly in a deep, deep reverie. How wise he looks—a grey, wise old water-hermit, with his head full of strange, unimaginable water-secrets, and strange, ancient water-memories. Perhaps he is—what was his name?— the god of streams himself, the old pagan god of streams, disguised as a frog for some wicked old pagan-godish adventure. Perhaps that 's why he is n't afraid of us—mere mortals. You 'd expect a mere frog to leap away or plunge under, would n't you?"

Again, for a second, she gave Anthony her eyes. They were filled with pensiveness and laughter.

In celebration of the sun's return, she wore a white frock (some filmy crinkled stuff, crêpe-de-chine perhaps), and carried a white sunshade, a thing all frills and furbelows. This she opened, as, leaving the shadow of the pines, she moved by the brook-side, down the lawn, where the unimpeded sun shone hot, towards the pond.

"The eighth wonder of the world—an olive-tree that bears roses," she remarked.

Her glance directed his to a gnarled old willow, growing by the pond. Indeed, with the wryness of its branches, the grey-green of its leaves, you might almost have mistaken it for an olive-tree. A rose-vine had clambered up to the topmost top of it, and spread in all directions, so that everywhere, vivid against the grey-green, hung red roses.

"And now, if you will come, I 'll show you the ninth wonder of the world," she promised. She led him down a long wide pathway, bordered on each side by hortensias in full blossom, two swelling hedges of fire, where purple dissolved into blue and crimson, blue into a hundred green, mauve, and violet overtones and undertones of blue, and crimson into every palest, vaguest, most elusive, and every intensest red the broken sunbeam bleeds upon the spectrum.

"But this," she said, "though you might well think it so, is not the ninth wonder of the world."

"I think the ninth wonder of the world, as well as the first and last, is walking beside me," said Anthony, in silence, to the sky.

The path ended in an arbour, roofed and walled with rose-vines; and herein were garden-chairs and a table.

"Shall we sit here a little?" proposed Susanna.

She put down her sunshade, and they established themselves under the roof of roses. On the table stood a Chinese vase, red and gold, with a dragon-handled cover.

"Occasion 's everything, beyond a doubt," thought Anthony. "But the rub is to know an occasion when you see it. Is *this* an occasion?"

He looked at her, and his heart trembled, and held him back.

"Oh, the fragrance of the roses," said Susanna. "How do they do it? A pinch of sunshine, a drop or two of dew, a puff of air, a handful of brown earth—and out of these they distil what seems as if it were the very smell of heaven."

But she spoke in tones noticeably hushed, as if fearing to be overheard.

Anthony looked round.

A moment ago there had not been a bird in sight (though, of course, the day was thridded through and through with the notes of those who were out of sight). But now, in the path before the arbour, all facing towards it, there must have been a score of birds—three or four sparrows, a pair of chaffinches, and then greenfinches, greenfinches, greenfinches. They were all facing expectantly towards the arbour, hopping towards it, hesitating, hopping on again, coming nearer, nearer.

Susanna, moving softly, lifted the dragon-handled cover from the Chinese vase. It was full of birdseed.

"Ah, I see," said Anthony. "Pensioners. But I suppose you have reflected that to give alms to the able-bodied is to pauperise them."

"Hush," she whispered, scorning his economics. "Please make yourself invisible, and be quiet."

Then, taking a handful of seed, and leaning forward, softly, softly she began to intone—

"Tu-ite, tu-ite,
Uccelli, fringuelli,
Passeri, verdonelli,
Venite, venite!"

and so, da capo, over and over again.

And the birds, hesitating, gaining confidence, holding back, hopping on, came nearer, nearer. A few, the boldest, entered the arbour . . . they all entered . . . they hesitated, hung back, hopped on. Now they were at her feet; now three were in her lap; others were on the table. On the table, in her lap, at her feet, she scattered seed. Then she took a second handful, and softly, softly, to a sort of lullaby tune,

"Perlino, Perlino,
Perlino Piumino,
Where is Perlino?
Come, Perlino,"

she sang, her open hand extended.

A greenfinch new up to the table, flew down to her knee, flew up to her shoulder, flew down to her hand, and, perching on her thumb, began to feed.

And she went on with her soft, soft intoning.

"This is Perlino,
So green, oh, so green, oh.
He is the bravest heart,
The sweetest singer, of them all.
I 'm obliged to impart my information
In the form of a chant;
For if I were to speak it out, prose-wise,
They would be frightened, they would fly away.
But I hope you admire
My fine contempt for rhyme and rhythm.
Is this not the ninth wonder of the world?
Would you or could you have believed,
If you had n't seen it?
That these wild birds,
Not the sparrows only,
But the shy, shy finches,
Could become so tame, so fearless?
Oh, it took time—and patience.
One had to come every day,
At the same hour,
And sit very still,
And softly, softly,
Monotonously, monotonously,
Croon, croon, croon,
As I am crooning now.
At first one cast one's seed
At a distance—
Then nearer, nearer,
Till at last—
Well, you see the result."

Her eyes laughed, but she was very careful not to move. Anthony, blotted against the leafy wall behind him, sat as still as a statue. Her eyes laughed. "Oh, such eyes!" thought he. Her red lips, smiling, took delicious curves. And the hand on which Perlino perched, with its slender fingers, its soft modelling, its warm whiteness, was like a thing carved of rose-marble and made alive.

"And Perlino," she resumed her chant—

"Perlino Piumino
Is the bravest of them all.
And now that he has made an end
Of his handful of seed,
I hope he will be so good
As to favour us with a little music.
Sometimes he will,
And sometimes he just obstinately won't.
Tu-ite, tu-ite, tu-ite,
Andiamo, Perlino, tu-ite!
Canta, di grazia, canta."

And after some further persuasion,—you will suspect me of romancing, but upon my word,—Perlino Piumino consented. Clinging to Susanna's thumb, he threw back his head, opened his bill, and poured forth his crystal song—a thin, bright, crystal rill, swift-flowing, winding in delicate volutions. And mercy, how his green little bosom throbbed.

"Is n't it incredible?" Susanna whispered. "It is wonderful to feel him. His whole body is beating like a heart."

And when his song was finished, she bent towards him, and—never, never so softly—touched the top of his green head with her lips.

"And, now—fly away, birdlings—back to your affairs," she said. "Good-bye until to-morrow."

She rose, and there was an instant whir of fluttering wings.

"Shall we walk?" she said to Anthony. She shook her frock, to dust the last grains of birdseed from it. "If we stay here, they will think there is more to come. And they 've had quite sufficient for one day."

She put up her sunshade, and they turned back into the alley of hortensias.

"You find me speechless," said Anthony. "Of course, it has n't really happened. But how—how do you produce so strong an illusion of reality? I could have sworn I saw a greenfinch feeding from your hand, I could have sworn I saw him cling there, and heard him sing his song. I could have sworn I saw you kiss him."

Susanna, under her white sunshade, laughed, softly, victoriously.

"Speaking with all moderation," he declared, "it is the most marvellous performance I have ever witnessed. If it had been a sparrow—or a pigeon—but—a greenfinch—!"

"There are very few birds that can't be tamed," she said. "You 've only got to familiarise them with your presence at a certain spot at a certain hour, and keep very still, and be very, very gentle in your movements, and croon to them, and bring them food. I have tamed wilder birds than greenfinches, in Italy—I have tamed goldfinches, blackcaps, and even an oriole. And if you have once tamed a bird, and made him your friend, he never forgets you. Season after season, when he returns from his migration, he recognises you, and takes up the friendship where it was put down. Until at last"—her voice sank, and she shook her head—"there comes a season when he returns no more."

They had strolled beyond the hortensias, into a shady avenue of elms. Round the trunk of one of these ran a circular bench. Susanna sat down. Anthony stood before her.

"I trust, at any rate," she said, whimsically smiling, "that the moral of my little exhibition has not been lost upon you?"

"A moral? Oh?" said he. "No. I had supposed it was beauty for beauty's sake."

"Ah, but beauty sometimes points a moral in spite of itself. The very obvious moral of this is that where there 's a will there 's a way."

She looked up, making her eyes grave; then smiled again.

"We must resume our plotting. I think I have found the way by which the Conte di Sampaolo can regain his inheritance."

Anthony laughed.

"There are exactly two ways by which he can do that," he said. "One is to equip an army, and go to war with the King of Italy, and—a mere detail—conquer him. The other is to procure a wishing-cap and wish it. Which do you recommend?"

"No," said Susanna. "There is a third and simpler way."

She was tracing patterns on the ground with the point of her parasol.

"There is the way of marriage."

She completed a circle, and began to draw a star within it.

"You should go to Sampaolo, and marry your cousin. So"—her eyes on her drawing, she spoke slowly, with an effect supremely impersonal—"so you would come to your own again; and so a house divided against itself, an ancient noble house, would be reunited; and an ancient historic line, broken for a little, would be made whole."

She put the fifth point to her star.

Anthony stood off, half laughing, and held up his hands, in admiring protest.

"Dear lady, what a programme!" was his laughing ejaculation.

"I admit," said she, critically regarding the figure at her feet, "that at first blush it may seem somewhat fantastic. But it is really worth serious consideration. You are the heir to a great name, which has been separated from the estates that are its appanage, and to a great tradition, which has been interrupted. But the heir to such a name, to such a tradition, is heir also to great duties, to great obligations. He has no right to be passive, or to think only of himself. The thirty-fourth Count of Sampaolo owes it to his thirty-three predecessors—the descendant of San Guido owes it to San Guido—to bestir himself, to do the very utmost in his power to revive and maintain the tradition. He is a custodian, a trustee. He has no right to sit down, idle and contented, to the life of a country gentleman in England. He is the banner-bearer of his race. He has no right to leave the banner folded in a dark closet. He must unfurl his banner, and bear it bravely in the sight of the world. That is the justification, that is the mission, of *noblesse*. A great nobleman should not evade or hide his nobility—he should bear it nobly in the sight of the world. That is the mission of the Conte di Sampaolo—that is the work he was born to do. It seems to me that at present he is pretty thoroughly neglecting his work."

She shot a smile at him, then lowered her eyes again upon her encircled star.

"You preach a very eloquent sermon," said Anthony, "and in principle I acknowledge its soundness. But in practice—there is just absolutely nothing the Conte di Sampaolo can do."

"He can go to Vallanza, and marry his cousin," reiterated she. "Thus the name and the estates would be brought together again, and the tradition would be renewed."

She had slipped a ring from her finger, and was vaguely playing with it.

Anthony only laughed.

"Does n't my proposition deserve better than mere laughter?" said she.

"I should laugh," said he, with secret meaning, "on the wrong side of my mouth, if I thought you wished me to take it seriously." ("If I thought she seriously wished me to marry another woman!" he breathed, shuddering, to his soul.)

"Why should n't I wish you to take it seriously?" she asked, studying her ring.

"The marriage of cousins is forbidden by Holy Church," said he.

"She 's only your second or third cousin. The nearest Bishop would give you a dispensation," answered Susanna, twirling her ring round in the palm of her hand.

"There would, of course, be no question of the lady rejecting me," he laughed.

"You would naturally endeavour to make yourself agreeable to her, and to capture her affections," she retorted, slipping the ring back upon its finger, and clasping her hands. "Besides, she could hardly be indifferent to the circumstance that you have it in your power to regularise her position. She calls herself the Countess of Sampaolo. She could do so with a clear conscience if she were the wife of the legitimate Count."

"She can do so with a clear conscience as it is," said Anthony. "She has the patent of the Italian King."

"Pinchbeck to gold," said Susanna. "A title improvised yesterday—and a title dating from 1104! The real thing, and a tawdry imitation. Go to Sampaolo, make her acquaintance, fall in love with her, persuade her to fall in love with you, marry her,—and there will be the grand old House of Valdeschi itself again."

Her eyes glowed.

But Anthony only laughed.

"You counsel procedures incompatible," he said. "If I am the custodian of a tradition, which you would have me maintain, how better could I play it false, than by marrying, of all women, the granddaughter, the heiress and representative, of the man who upset it?"

"You would heal a family feud, and blot out a wrong," said she, drawing patterns again with her sunshade. "Magnanimity should be *part* of your tradition. You would not visit the sins of the fathers upon the children? You don't hold your cousin personally responsible?"

She looked up obliquely at him.

"Personally," he answered, "my cousin may be the most innocent soul alive. She is born to a ready-made situation, and accepts it. But it is a situation which I, if I am to be loyal to my tradition, cannot accept. It is the negation of my tradition. I am obliged to submit to it, but I can't accept it.

My cousin is the embodiment of the anti-tradition. You say—marry her. That is like inviting the Pope to ally himself with the Antipope."

"No, no," contended Susanna, arresting her sunshade in the midst of an intricate vermiculation. "For the Antipope must be in wilful personal rebellion; while your cousin is what she is, quite independently of her own will—perhaps in spite of it. Imagine me, for instance, in her place—me," she smiled, "the sole legitimist in Sampaolo. What could I do? I find myself in possession of stolen goods. I would, if I could, restore them at once to their rightful owner. But I can't—because I am only the tenant for life. I can't sell them, nor give them away, nor even, dying, dispose of them by will. I am only the tenant for life. After me, they must pass to the next heir. So, if I wish to restore them to their rightful owner, there 's but a single means of doing so open to me—I must induce the rightful owner to make me his wife."

She smiled again, mirthfully, but with conviction, with conclusiveness, as who should say, "I have proved my point."

"Ah," pronounced Anthony, with stress, though perhaps a trifle ambiguously, "if it were you, it would be different."

"In your cousin's case, to be sure," pursued Susanna, "there is one other means. You happen to be, on the Valdeschi side, her nearest kinsman, and therefore, until she marries and has children, you are her heir presumptive. Well, if she were to retire into a convent, taking vows of celibacy and poverty, then what they call the usufruct of her properties could be settled upon her heir presumptive for her lifetime, the properties themselves passing to him at her death."

"We will wish the young lady no such dreary fate," laughed Anthony. "Fortunately for her, she is not troubled by your scruples."

"How do you know she is n't?" asked Susanna.

"We can safely take it for granted," said he. "Besides, you have told me so yourself."

"*I* have told you so—?" she puzzled.

"You have told me that there is but one legitimist in Sampaolo. If my cousin were troubled by your scruples, she would make a second. And of the whole population of the island, can you suggest a less probable second?"

"They say that Queen Anne was at heart a Jacobite," Susanna reminded him. "Your cousin is young. One could lay the case before her, one could work upon her conscience. And, supposing her conscience to be once roused, then, if you could n't be brought to offer her your hand, she 'd have no choice but renunciation and the Cloister."

"Let us hope, therefore, that her conscience may remain comfortably asleep," said he. "For even to save her from the Cloister, I could not offer her my hand."

Susanna, leaning back against the rugged trunk of her elm, gazed down the long shaded avenue, and appeared to muse. Here and there, the sun, finding a way through the green cloud of leaves, a visible fillet of light in the dim atmosphere, dappled the brown earth with rose. In her white frock, her dark hair loose about her brow, a faint colour in her cheeks, her dark eyes musing, musing but half smiling at the same time, I think she looked very charming, very interesting, very warmly and richly feminine, I think she looked very lovely, very lovable; and I don't wonder that Anthony—as his eyes rested upon her, fed upon her—felt something violent happen in his heart.

"Occasion is everything—the occasion has come—the occasion has come," a silent voice seemed to incite him. And as it were unseen hands seemed to push him on.

The blood rushed tumultuously to his head.

"I 'm going to risk it, I 'm going to risk everything," he decreed, suddenly, recklessly.

"There are a thousand reasons why I could not offer her my hand," he said. "One reason is that I am in love with another woman."

His throat was dry, his voice sounded strained. His heart beat hard. He had burned his first bridge. He kept his eyes on her.

She continued to gaze down the avenue. I think she caught her breath, though.

"Oh—?" she said, after an instant, on a tone that tried in vain to be a tone of conventional politeness. She had been perfectly aware, of course, that it was bound to come. She had fancied herself perfectly prepared to cope with it, when it should come. But she had not expected it to come just yet. It took her off her guard.

"Yes," said he; "and you know whom I am in love with."

This time there could be no doubt that she caught her breath. She had overestimated her power of self-command, her talent for dissembling. She had known that it was bound to come; she had imagined that she could meet it lightly, humorously, that she could parry it, and never betray herself. And here she was, catching her breath, whilst her heart trembled and sank and sang within her. She bit her lip, in vexation; she closed her eyes, in ecstasy; she kept her face turned down the avenue, in fear.

Anthony's heart was leaping. A wild hope had kindled in it.

"I am in love with *you*—with *you*," he cried, in a voice that shook.

She did not speak, she did not look at him, but she caught her breath audibly, a long tremulous breath.

He knelt at her feet, he seized her hands. She did not withdraw them.

"I love you, I love you. Don't keep your face turned from me. Look at me. Answer me. I love you. Will you marry me?"

He felt her hands tremble in his. Her surrender of them—was it not fuel to the fire of his hope? He put his lips to them, he kissed them, he covered them with kisses. They were warm, and sweet to smell, faintly, terribly sweet to smell.

At last she drew them away. She shrunk away herself, back along her bench. She bit her lip, in chagrin at her weakness, her self-indulgence. She knew that she was losing ground, precious, indispensable, to that deep-laid, secret, cherished plot of hers. But her heart sang and sang, but a joy such as she had never dreamed of filled it. Oh, she had known that her heart would be filled with joy, when he should say, "I love you"; but she had never dreamed of a joy such as this. This was a joy the very elements of which were new to her; different, not in degree only, but in kind, from any joy she had experienced before. She could not so soon put it by, she could not yet bid herself be stern.

"Look at me. Answer me. I love you. Will you marry me?" he cried.

But she *must* bid herself be stern. "I must, I must," she thought. She made a mighty effort.

"No," she said, in a suffocated voice, painfully.

"Oh, look at me," he pleaded. "Why do you keep your face turned away? Why do you say no? I love you. Will you marry me? Say yes, say yes."

But she did not look at him.

"No. I can't. Don't ask me," she said.

"Why can't you? I love you. I adore you. Why should n't I ask you?"

The palest flicker of a smile passed over her face.

"I want you to marry your cousin," she said.

"Is that the only reason?"

"Is n't that a sufficient reason?"

Again there was the flicker of a smile.

"For heaven's sake, look at me. Don't keep your face turned away. Then you don't—you don't care for me—not an atom?"

"I"—she could not deny herself one instant of weakness more, one supreme instant; afterwards she would be stern in earnest, she would draw back—"I never meant to let you know I did."

And for the first time between two heart-beats her eyes met his, stayed with his.

For the time between two heart-beats, Time stood still, the world stood still, Time and the world ceased to be. Her eyes stayed with his. There was nothing else in all created space but her two eyes, her soft and deep, dark and radiant eyes. Far, far within them shone a light. Her soul came forth from its hiding place, and shining far, far within her eyes, showed itself to his soul, yielded itself to his soul.

"Then you do—you do," he cried. It was almost a wail. The universe reeled round him.

He had sprung to his feet. He threw himself on the bench beside her, facing her. He seized her hands again. He tried again to get her eyes.

"No, no, no," she said, freeing her hands, shrinking from him. "No. I don't—I don't."

"But you do. You said you did. You—you showed that you did."

He waited, triumphant, anxious, breathless.

"No, no, no. I did n't say it—I did n't mean it."

"But you did mean it. Your eyes . . ."

But when he remembered her eyes, speech deserted him. He could only gasp and tingle.

"No, no, no," she said. "I meant nothing. Please—please don't come so near. Stand up—there" (her hand indicated where), "and we will speak of it—reasonably."

Her hand remained suspended, enjoining obedience.

Anthony, perplexed, dashed a little, obeyed, and stood before her.

"We must be reasonable," she said. "I meant nothing. If I seemed moved, it was because—oh, because I was so taken by surprise, I suppose."

She was getting herself in hand. She looked at him quite fearlessly now, with eyes that pretended to forget they had ever been complaisant.

"The Count of Sampaolo," she argued calmly, "is not free to marry whom he will. He has his inheritance to regain, his mission to fulfil. I will never allow myself to be made an obstacle to that. He must marry no one but his cousin. I will never stand between him and her—between him and what is equally his interest and his duty."

But Anthony, too, was getting himself in hand.

"Look here," he said, with some peremptoriness. "You may just once for all eliminate my cousin from your calculations. I beg you to understand that even if you did n't exist, there could be no question of my cousin. No earthly consideration could induce me to make any sort of terms with that branch of my family—let alone a marriage. So!" A wave of the hand dismissed his cousin for ever to Crack-limbo. "But as you do exist, and as I happen to love you, and as I happen to have discovered—what I could never wildly have dared to hope—that you are not utterly indifferent to me, I may tell you that I intend to marry *you*—*you*—*you*. You imperial, adorable woman! You!"

Susanna hastily turned her eyes down the avenue.

"In fact," Anthony added, with serene presumption, "I have the honour to apprise you of our engagement."

She could n't repress a nervous little laugh. Then she rose.

"They 'll be expecting me at the house," she said, and moved in that direction.

"I 'm waiting for your congratulations," said he, walking beside her.

She gave another little laugh. And neither spoke again until they had reached the hall door, which he opened for her.

"Well?" he asked.

"Come back after luncheon," said she. "Come back at three o'clock—and
I will tell you something."

XVI

"Own up—and name the day," said Miss Sandus, when she had heard Susanna's story. "There 's nothing left for you to do, my dear, but to make a clean breast of it, and name the happy day."

They were in the billiard-room, after luncheon. Miss Sandus was sipping coffee, while Susanna, cue in hand, more or less absently knocked about the balls. So that their remarks were punctuated by an erratic series of ivory *toc-tocs*.

"I 'm afraid if I own up," she answered, "there won't be any happy day. He swore that no earthly consideration could induce him to make any sort of terms with my branch of the family. Those were his very words."

Toc—she pocketed the red.

"Fudge," pronounced Miss Sandus. "Capital words for eating. He 'll gobble, he 'll bolt 'em. Give him the chance. It's astonishing how becoming it is to you young women to play billiards, how it brings out the grace of your blessed figures. Say, 'I, even I, am your cousin. Do you still decline to marry her?'—and see what he 'll do. No, no—you want to take it a little more to the right and lower down. That's it." (*Toc-toc*—Susanna made a cannon.) "He 'll jump at you. I know the man. There 's no possible question of it. So I must be thinking of the gown I 'm to wear as bridesmaid."

She laughed, and put down her cup.

Susanna, trying for another cannon, fluked another pocket.

"No," she said. "That would be to miss half the fun of the situation. The thing must be more dramatic. Besides, I want it to happen at Sampaolo. I want him to go to Sampaolo. And I want to tempt him and test him.

"'Not so, said she, but I will see
If there be any faith in man.'"

she quoted (or misquoted?—I forget). "He shall go to Sampaolo and be tempted. With his own eyes he shall behold the heritage of the Valdeschi. Then he shall be approached by his cousin's friends,—by the reluctant but obedient Commendatore Fregi, for example,—and sorely tempted. I 've got rather a subtle little scheme. I 'll explain it to you later—he 'll be arriving at any moment now. He shall leave for Sampaolo to-morrow morning. You and I will leave the morning after, if you please. Only, of course, he's to know nothing about that—he's to suppose that we 're remaining here."

She attempted a somewhat delicate stroke off the cushion, and achieved it.

"Good shot," approved Miss Sandus. "But you are forgetting Mr. Willes. Mr. Willes will tell him."

"No, I 've not forgotten Mr. Willes," said Susanna. "I should n't very much mind letting Mr. Willes into my confidence. But I think on the whole I 'll make him take Mr. Willes with him."

"You 're nothing if not arbitrary," Miss Sandus laughed.

"I come of a line of tyrants," said Susanna. "And, anyhow, what's the good of possessing power, if you 're not to exercise and enjoy it?"

The clock on the mantelpiece began to strike three.

"Mr. Craford," announced a servant.

Miss Sandus fled from the room by a French window.

Susanna returned her cue to the rack.

XVII

Anthony had passed, I imagine, the longest hour and a half that he had ever passed, or will ever be likely to pass: the longest, the most agitated, the most elated, the most impatient.

Could he regard himself as accepted? Well, certainly, as the next thing to it. And, in any case, she had confessed that she cared for him.

"I never meant to let you know I did."

Oh, he heard it again and again. Again and again her eyes met his, as they had met them at that consummate moment, discovering her soul to him. Again and again he knelt before her, and kissed her hands, warm and soft, and sweet with that faint perfume which caused cataclysms in his heart.

He went home, he went in to luncheon. Somehow he must wear out the time till three o'clock.

"Come back at three o'clock—and I will tell you something."

What had she to tell him? What would he hear when he went back at three o'clock? Here was a question for hope and fear to play about.

Adrian prattled merrily over the luncheon table. I wonder how many of his words Anthony took in.

After luncheon he tramped about the park, counting the slow minutes,—kissing her hands, looking into her eyes, racking his brain with speculations as to what she might have to tell him, hoping, fearing, and counting the long slow minutes. And his tug at Susanna's doorbell coincided with the very first stroke of three from her billiard-room clock.

His throat was dry, his pulses pounded, his knees all but knocked together under him, as he followed the manservant across the hall, into her presence.

XVIII

Susanna returned her cue to the rack.

Anthony stood near the door, an incarnate question.

"Well—?" he demanded, in a voice that was tense.

"Come in," she amiably welcomed him. "Sit down."

She pointed to a chair. She wore the same white frock that she had worn before luncheon, only she had stuck a red rose in her belt.

He did n't sit down, but he came forward, and stood by the fireplace.

"What an age, what an eternity it has been," he profoundly sighed. "I have grown grey waiting for this instant."

She studied him, with amusement.

"The grey is very skilfully concealed," she remarked.

"The grey is in my soul," said he, with the accent of tragedy. "Well—?" he again demanded.

"Well what?" teased she, arching her eye-brows innocently.

"Oh, come," he remonstrated. "Don't torture a defenceless animal. Seal my fate, pronounce my doom. I love you—love you—love you. Will you have me?"

She stood silhouetted against a window, the light sifting and shining through her hair.

"I have a condition to make," she said. "You must promise to comply with my condition—and then I can answer you."

Her dark eyes smiled into his, quizzically, but perhaps with a kind of tenderness too.

He came nearer.

"A condition? What's the condition?"

"No—you must promise first to agree to it," she said.

"A promise in the dark?" he objected.

"Oh, if you can't trust me!" she cried, with a little shrug.

"There's mischief in your eye," said he. "The man deserves what he gets, who makes promises in the dark."

"Then make the promise—and see whether you get what you deserve," she laughed.

"Mercy forbid that any man should get what he deserves," said he. "I am a suppliant for grace, not justice."

Susanna laughed again. She took her rose from her belt, and brushed her face with it, touched it with her lips.

"Do you care for roses?" she asked, with a glance of intellectual curiosity, as one who spoke solely for the purpose of acquiring knowledge.

"I should care for that rose," said he, vehemently.

She held it out to him, still laughing, but with a difference.

He seized the rose—and suddenly, over-mastered by his impulse, suddenly, violently, made towards her.

But she drew away, extending her hands to protect herself.

"I beg your pardon," he said, pulling himself up. "But you should make a conscientious effort to be a trifle less adorable."

He pressed her rose to his mouth, crushing it, breathing in its scent, trying to possess himself of the touch her mouth had left upon it.

She sank into the corner of a sofa, and leaned back among the cushions.

"Well, do you promise?" she asked, smiling up at him.

"Do you flatter yourself that you 're a trifle less adorable now?" asked he, smiling down.

"Do you promise?" she repeated, taking away her eyes.

"I clean forget what it was you wished me to promise," said he.

"You are to promise to comply with my condition. Do you?"

"I suppose I must," he answered, with a gesture of submission.

"But do you? You must say"—she made her voice sepulchral—"'I solemnly do.'"

She gave him her eyes again, held him with them.

He was rigid for a minute, gazing fixedly at her.

"I solemnly do," he said at last, relaxing. "What's the condition?"

"The condition is an easy one—only a little journey to make."

"A journey to make? Away from Craford?"

He stood off, suspicious, prepared to be defiant.

"Yes," said she, playing with the lace of one of her cushions.

"Not for worlds," said he. "Anything else. But I won't leave Craford."

"You have promised," said she.

"Ah, but I did n't dream there would be any question of my leaving Craford. There's a woman at Craford I 'm in love with. I won't leave Craford."

"You have solemnly promised," said she.

"Hang my promise," gaily he outfaced her.

"Promises are sacred." She looked serious.

"Not promises extorted in the dark," contended he.

"Give me back my rose," said she, putting forth her hand.

"No," said he, pressing the rose anew to his face.

"Yes," said she, her foolhardy hand awaiting it.

For, instead of giving her back her rose, he threw himself upon her hand, and had kissed it before she could catch it away.

She bit her lip, frowning, smiling.

"Then will you keep your promise?" she asked severely.

"If you insist upon it, I suppose I 'll have to," he grudgingly consented. "But a journey!" he sighed. "Ah, well. Where to?"

Her eyes gleamed, maliciously.

"To a very pleasant place," she said. "The journey is a pious pilgrimage."

"Craford, just now, is the only pleasant place on the face of the earth," vowed he. "A pious pilgrimage? Where to?"

He had, I think, some vague notion that she might mean a pilgrimage to the Holy Well of St. Winefride in Wales; though, for that matter, why not to the Holy Well of St. Govor in Kensington Gardens?

"A pious pilgrimage to the home of your ancestors," said Susanna. "The journey is a journey to the little, unknown, beautiful island of Sampaolo."

Her eyes gleamed, maliciously, exultantly.

But Anthony fell back, aghast.

"Sampaolo?" he cried.

"Yes," said she, quietly.

"Oh, I say!" He writhed, he groaned. "That is too much. Really!"

"That is my condition," said Susanna. Her mouth was firm.

"You don't mean it—you can't mean it." He frowned his incredulity.

"I mean it literally," she persisted. "You must make a journey to Sampaolo."

"But what's the *sense* of it?" he besought her. "Why on earth should you *impose* such a condition?" He frowned his incomprehension.

"Because you have asked me to be your wife," she answered.

He shook his head, mournfully, scornfully.

"If ever an explanation darkened counsel!" mournfully he jeered.

"You have asked me to be your wife. I reply that first you must make a journey to Sampaolo. Is that not simple?" said Susanna.

He was walking about the room.

"Do you mean to say "—he came to a standstill—"that if I make a journey to Sampaolo, you *will* be my wife?"

"I mean to say that I will never be your wife unless you do."

"But if I do—?"

She leaned back, smiling, among her cushions.

"That will depend upon the result of your journey."

He shook his head again.

"I 'm utterly at sea," he professed. "I have never heard anything that sounded so bewilderingly devoid of reason. Explain yourself. What is it all about?"

"Reflect for a moment," said she, assuming a tone argumentative. "Consider the embarrassment of my position. You ask me to be your wife. But if I consent, you give up your only chance of regaining your Italian patrimony—do you not? But a man should at least *know* what he is giving up. *You* should know what your patrimony consists of. You should know, as the saying is, what you 'stand to lose.' Therefore you must go to Sampaolo, and see it with your own eyes. Isola Nobile, Castel San Guido, the Palazzo Rosso, Villa Formosa—you must see them all, with their gardens and their pictures and their treasures. And then you must ask yourself in cold blood, 'Is that woman I left at Craford really worth it?'"

She smiled. But, as he made to speak, her hand commanded silence.

"No, no," she said. "You have not seen them yet, so you can't tell. When you have seen them, you will very likely thank me for leaving you free to-day. You will think, with a shudder, 'Good heavens, what a narrow escape! What if she had taken me at my word?' Then you can offer yourself to your cousin, and let us hope she 'll accept you."

Again, as he made to speak, her hand silenced him.

"But if," she went on, "if, by any chance, you should *not* thank me,—if, in cold blood, with your eyes open, you should decide that the woman you left at Craford *is* worth it,—why, then you can return to her, and renew your suit. And she'll have the satisfaction of knowing that *you* know what's she costing you."

Anthony stood over her, looked down upon her.

"This is the most awful nonsense," he said, with a grave half-laugh.

"It is my condition," said she. "You must start for Sampaolo to-morrow morning."

"You 'll never really send me on such a fool's errand," he protested.

"You have promised," said she.

"You won't hold me to the promise."

"If I release you from it," she warned him, her eyes becoming dangerous, "there must be no more talk of marriage between you and me."

He flung away from her, and resumed his walk about the room. He gazed distressfully into space, as if appealing to invisible arbiters.

"This is too childish—and too cruel," he complained. "I 'm not an idiot. I don't need an object-lesson. I am not utterly without imagination. I can see Sampaolo with my mind's eye. And seeing it, I decide in cold blood that not for forty million Sampaolos would I give up the woman I adore. There—I 've made the journey, and come back. Now I renew my suit. Will you have me?"

He stood over her again.

"There must be no more talk of having or not having between you and me—till you have kept your promise," said Susanna, coldly avoiding his gaze.

Anthony clenched his fists, ground his teeth.

"What folly—what obstinacy—what downright wanton capriciousness," in anger he muttered.

"And yet, two minutes ago, this man said he loved me," Susanna murmured, meaningly, to the ceiling.

"If I were n't unfortunate enough to love you, I should n't mind your—your perfectly barbarous unkindness."

He glared at her. But she met his glare with a smile that disarmed it. And, in spite of himself, he smiled too.

"Will you start to-morrow?" she asked, softly, coaxingly.

"This is outrageous," he said. "How long do you expect me to stay?"

"Oh, for that," she considered, "I shall be very moderate. A week will do. A diligent sightseer should be able to see Sampaolo pretty thoroughly in a week."

"A week," he calculated, "and I suppose one must allow at least another week for getting there and back. So you exile me for a fortnight?"

His tone and his eyes pleaded with her.

"A fortnight is not much," said she, lightly.

"No," he gloomily acquiesced. "It is only fourteen lifetimes to a man who happens to be in love."

"Men are reputed to be stronger than women," she reproached him, with a look. "If a mere woman can stand a fortnight——!"

Anthony gasped—and sprang towards her.

"No, no," she cried, shrinking away.

"Do *you* happen to be in love?" he said, restraining himself.

She looked at him very kindly.

"I will tell you that, when you come back—*if* you come back," she promised.

"*If* I come back!" he derided. Then, with eagerness, "You will write to me? I may write to you?" he stipulated.

"Oh, no—by no means. There must be no sort of communication between us. You must give yourself every chance to forget me—and to think of your cousin."

"I won't go," said Anthony.

He planted himself in a chair, facing her, and assumed the air of a fixture.

But Susanna rose.

"Good-bye, then," she said, and held out her hand.

"What do you mean?" said he.

But he took her hand, and kept it.

"All is over between us—if you won't go."

But she left her hand in his.

"You *will* write to me?"

He caressed the warm soft fingers.

"No."

"But I *may* write to you?"

He kissed the fragrant fingers.

At last, slowly, gently, she drew her hand away.

"Oh, if it will give you any satisfaction to write to me, I suppose you may," she conceded. "But remember—you must n't expect your letters to be answered."

She went back to her place in the corner of the sofa.

He left his chair, and stood over her again.

"I love you," he said.

She smiled and played with the lace of her cushion.

"So you remarked before," she said.

"I love you," said he, with fervour.

"By the bye," she said, "I forgot to mention that you are to take Mr. Willes with you."

"Oh—?" puzzled Anthony. "Willes? Why?"

"For several reasons," said Susanna. "But will one suffice?"

"What's the one?"

She looked up at him, and laughed.

"Because I wish it."

Anthony laughed too.

"You are conscious of your power," he said.

"Yes," she admitted. "So you will take Mr. Willes?"

"You have said you wished it."

And then, for a while, neither spoke, but I fancy their eyes carried on the conversation.

XIX

It was nearly time to dress for dinner when Anthony returned to Craford
Old Manor.

Adrian, his collar loosened, his hair towzled, his head cocked critically to one side, was in his business-room, seated at his piano, playing over and over again a single phrase, and now and then making a little alteration in it, which he would hurriedly jot down in a manuscript music-book, laid open on a table at his elbow.

"Are n't you going for a holiday this summer?" Anthony asked, with languor, lounging in.

"Hush-sh-sh!" said Adrian, intent upon his manuscript, waving an admonitory hand.

"It's time to dress," said Anthony. He lighted a cigarette.

Adrian strummed through his phrase again, brows knitted, looking intensely judicial. Then he swung round on his piano-stool.

"Hey? What did you say?" he questioned, his blue eyes vague, his pink face blank.

"I merely asked whether you were n't going for a holiday this summer," Anthony repeated, between two outputs of smoke.

"And you interrupt a heaven-sent musician, when you see the fit's upon him, merely to ask an irrelevant thing like that," Adrian reproved him. "I was holding an assize, a gaol-delivery. That phrase was on trial before me for its life. In art, sir, one should imitate the methods of a hanging judge. Put every separate touch on trial for its life, and deem it guilty till it can prove itself innocent. Yea, even though these same touches be dear to you as her children to a mother. Such is the high austerity of art. I thought you said it was time to dress."

"So it is," said Anthony. "Are n't you going for a holiday this summer?"

Adrian closed his music-book, and got up.

"Of course I am," he answered.

"When?" said Anthony.

"In September, as usual," said Adrian.

"I was wondering," said Anthony, twiddling his cigarette, "whether you would mind taking your holiday a little earlier than usual this year—in August, for instance?"

"Why?" asked Adrian, with caution.

"It would suit me better, I could spare you better," Anthony said.

Adrian eyed him suspiciously.

"In August? We 're in August now, are n't we?"

"I believe so," said Anthony. "Either August or late July. One could find out from the almanac, I suppose. It would suit me very well if you could take your holiday now—at once."

Adrian's suspicion became acute.

"What are you up to? What do you want to get rid of *me* for?"

Anthony smoked.

"I don't want to get rid of you. On the contrary—I 'll go with you, if you like."

Adrian scrutinized him searchingly, suspicion reinforced by astonishment. All at once his eyes flashed.

"Aha!" he cried. "I see what you 've been at. You 've been trying to philander with the Nobil Donna Susanna Torrebianca—and she 's sent you about your business. Oh, *I 've* seen how things were going." He winked and nodded.

"Nothing of the sort," said Anthony. "You might tell Wickersmith to pack our things. We 'll take the eight-fifteen up to-morrow morning. That will get us to Victoria in time for the eleven o'clock Continental express."

"Oh? We 're going abroad?" asked Adrian.

"I suppose so. Where else is there to go?" said Anthony.

"I could have told you beforehand," Adrian consoled him, "that you had n't the ghost of a chance with her. You grim, glum, laconic sort of men are n't at all the sort that would appeal to a rich, poetic, southern nature like Madame Torrebianca's. She would be attracted by an exuberant, expansive, warm, sunny sort of man,—a man genial and fruity, like old wine,—sweet and tender and mellow, like ripe peaches. If it were n't that I sternly discountenance the imperilling of business interests by mixing them up with personal sentiment, I should very probably have paid court to her myself. And now I expect you have lost me a tenant. I expect she 'll not care to renew the lease."

"Don't know, I 'm sure," said Anthony. "You might ask her. We 're dining with her to-night. That would make a graceful dinner-table topic."

Adrian's blue eyes grew round.

"We 're dining with her to-night?"

That did n't at all fit his theory of the case.

"At least I am," affirmed Anthony, dropping the end of his cigarette into an ash-tray. "And she said I might bring you, if you 'd promise to be good."

"*The—deuce*!" ejaculated Adrian, in something between a whisper and a whistle. "But—then—why—what—what under the sun are you going abroad for?"

"A mere whim—a sheer piece of perversity—a sleeveless errand," Anthony answered. "So now we might set about sweeping and garnishing ourselves," he suggested, moving towards the door.

Susanna was very beautiful, I think, in a rose-coloured dinner-gown (rose-coloured chiffon, with accessories of drooping old pale-yellowish lace), a spray of scarlet geranium in her hair, pearls round her throat, and, as you could now and then perceive, high-heeled scarlet slippers on her feet.

She was very beautiful, very pleasant and friendly; and if she seemed, perhaps, a thought less merry, a thought more pensive, than her wont—if sometimes, for a second or two, she seemed to lose herself, while her eyes gazed far away, and her lips remained slightly parted—I doubt if Anthony liked her any the less for this.

But what he pined for was a minute alone with her; and that appeared to be by no means forthcoming. After dinner they all went out upon the terrace, where it was lighted by the open French windows of the drawing-room, and reposed in wicker chairs, whilst they sipped their coffee. He looked at her, and his heart grew big—with grief, with resentment, with delight, with despair, with hope. "She cares for me—she has said it, she has shown it. But then why does she send me on this egregious wild-goose chase? She cares for me. But then why does n't she arrange to give me a minute alone with her to-night?"

In the end,—well, was it Adrian, or was it Miss Sandus, whom he had to thank for their minute alone?

"Why does nobody say, 'Dear kind Mr. Willes, do be nice, and sing us something'?" Adrian plaintively inquired.

Anthony grasped the skirts of happy chance.

"Dear kind Mr. Willes, do be nice, and sing us something," he said at once.

"I 'll play your accompaniments," volunteered Miss Sandus.

And she and the songster went into the drawing-room.

"Thank heaven," said Anthony, under his breath, but fervently, gazing hard at Susanna.

She gave a little laugh.

"What are you laughing at?" he asked.

"At your sudden access of piety," said she.

"At any rate," said he, "I owe no thanks to *you*. For all you cared, apparently, we should have spent the whole of this last precious evening surrounded by strangers."

"Mamam, dites-moi ce qu'on sent
Quand on aime,"

came the voice of Adrian from within.

"If you talk, we can't hear the music," said Susanna.

"Bother the music," responded Anthony.

"It was you who asked him to sing," she said.

"Bother his singing. This is my last evening with you. Do you think a woman has the right to be as gloriously beautiful as you are to-night? Do you think it's fair to the feelings of a poor wretched man, who adores her, and whom she, in mere wanton wickedness, is sending to the uttermost ends of the earth?"

Susanna had her fan of white feathers in her lap. She caressed it.

"I want to ask you something," said Anthony.

"What is it?" said she.

"A piece of information, to help me on my journey. Will you give it me?"

"If I can, of course," said she, putting her fan on the table.

"You promise?" said he.

"If I have any information that can be of use to you, I 'll give it with pleasure," she agreed.

"Very good. That's a promise," said he. "Now then, for my question. I love you. Do you love me?"

He looked hard at her.

She laughed, in acknowledgment that she had been fairly caught. Then her eyes softened.

"Yes," she said.

But before he could move, she had sprung up, and disappeared through one of the French windows, joining Miss Sandus and Adrian at the piano.

In her flight, however, she forgot her fan. It lay where she had left it on the table.

Anthony picked it up, pressed it to his face. He closed his eyes, and kept it pressed to his face. Its fragrance was more than a mere fragrance—there was something of herself in it, something poignantly, intimately personal.

By and by he put the fan in his pocket, in the inside pocket of his coat—feathers downwards, the better to conceal it. Then he too joined the group at the piano.

XX

In their sitting-room in the Hôtel de Rome, at Vallanza, Anthony and Adrian were waiting for their breakfast. It is evident, therefore, that Susanna's will had prevailed, and a fool's errand was in process of accomplishment. The fool, no doubt, to the last moment, had renewed his protests, his pleadings, his refusals; but, at each fresh outburst, coldly, firmly, the lady had reiterated her ultimatum, "Then all is over between you and me." And in the end, very conscious of his folly, very much incensed by her perversity, disgusted, dejected, and, as his travelling-companion had occasion to observe, in the very devil of a temper, he had left Victoria by the eleven o'clock Continental express. "Never forget," Miss Sandus whispered in his ear, as he paid her his adieux, "never forget that sound old adage—'journeys end in lovers meeting.'" This was oracular, and he had no opportunity to press for an interpretation; but it was clearly intended as of good omen. At the same time, in another part of the room, Susanna was whispering to Adrian. As Adrian never again expressed the slightest curiosity anent the motive of their hegira, I am led to wonder whether Susanna had admitted him to her confidence. She had intimated that she should n't especially mind doing so; and it is certain that he, from that time forth, now and then smiled at the sky with an eye that looked very knowing.

Those who have recently visited Sampaolo will remember the Hôtel de Rome as a small, new, spick-and-span establishment, built at the corner of the Piazza San Guido and the Riva Vittorio Emmanuele, and presenting none of that "local colour in the shape of dirt and discomfort" which we are warned to expect in Italy, if we depart from the track beaten by the tourist. I am told that the modern Italian commercial gentleman (who is often a German, and not infrequently a Jew) has learned some of the tourist's exactions. It is thanks to him, presumably, that even at out-of-the-way Vallanza there exists a decent inn.

Our friends' sitting-room was on the first floor, a corner room, having two sets of windows. One set commanded the Piazza, with its grey old church (the Cathedral of St. Paul and St. Guy), its detached campanile, its big central fountain, and, occupying the entire eastern side, the crumbling frescoed front of the Palazzo Rosso. The other set looked across the Riva, and its double row of palms, out upon the bay, with its anchored ships, its fishing-boats, its encircling olive-covered hills, dotted high and low by villages and villas, and its embosomed Islets, Isola Nobile, Isola Fratello, Isola Sorella, the whole wide prospect glowing in the sun.

The Piazza, which opens to the north, lay in cool blue shadow; and just now a market was in progress there, a jumble-scene of merchandise, animals, and humanity; men, women, and children, dogs and donkeys, goats, calves, pigs, poultry; vegetables and fruit—quartered melons, with green rind, black seeds, and rosy flesh, great golden pumpkins, onions in festoons, figs in pyramids; boots, head-gear, and rough shop-made clothing, for either sex; cheap jewellery also; and every manner of requisite for the household, from pots and pans of wrought copper, brass lamps, iron bedsteads and husk-filled bedding, to portraits in brilliant oleograph of King and Queen and the inevitable Garibaldi. The din was stupendous. Humanity hawked, chaffered, haggled, laughed, vituperated. Donkeys brayed, calves mooed, dogs barked, ducks quacked, pigs squealed. A dentist had set up his chair near the fountain, and was brawling proffers of relief to the tooth-distressed. Sometimes a beglamoured sufferer would allow himself to be taken in hand; and therewith, above the general blare and blur of noise, rose clear and lusty a series of shameless Latin howls. The town-crier, in a cocked hat, wandered hither and thither, like a soul in pain, feebly beating his drum, and droning out a nasal proclamation to which, so far as was apparent, no one listened. The women, for the most part, wore bright-coloured skirts,—striped green and red, or blue and yellow,—and long black veils, covering the head, and falling below the waist; the men, dark jerseys, corduroy trousers, red belts in lieu of braces, and red fishers' caps with tassels that dangled over the ear. Two such men, at this moment, passed up the Piazza arm-in-arm, singing. I don't know what their song was, but they had good voices, and while one of them carried the melody, the other sang a second.

Anthony, morose and listless, Adrian, all agog with excitement, had been looking down upon this spectacle for some minutes in silence. It was their first glimpse of daylit Sampaolo. They had arrived from Venice last night after dark.

But now, as the men passed singing, Adrian was moved to utterance.

"Italia, oh, Italia!" he exclaimed. "I thought I knew my Italy. I thought I had visited my Italy every year or two, for more years than you could shake a stick at. But this is too Italian to be true. This is not Italy—this is Italian opera."

Anthony gloomed.

"It's an infernal bore, whatever it is," he declared.

"Fie, fie," Adrian chid him. "Infernal? That is not at all a nice word. Don't let me hear it a second time. How animated and southern and picturesque that *arracheur-de-dents* is, is n't he? What distinction he confers upon the scene. Have you no teeth that need attending to? I should love to see you operated on by a practitioner like that, in the fresh air, under the azure canopy of heaven, in the eye of the world, fearless and unashamed. The long, rather rusty building opposite, with the pictures fading from its walls, is none other than the Palazzo Rosso, the cradle of your race. It can be visited between ten and four. I 've had a talk with our landlord's daughter—such a pretty girl. Her name—what do you suppose her name is? Her name is Pia. She has nice hair and eyes, and is a perfect cornucopia of information.—Ah, at last!" he sighed, pressing his hand to his heart, as the door opened, and the waiter appeared, bearing a tray.

Then, as the waiter set out the contents of his tray upon the table, Adrian, bending forward, examined them with the devoutness, with the intentness, of an impassioned connoisseur.

"Grilled ham, gallantine of chicken *aux truffes*, mortadella, an omelette *aux fines herbes*, coffee, hot milk, whipped cream, bread, figs, apricots," he enumerated. "And if it had n't been for my talk with the landlord's daughter, do you know what we should have had? We should have had coffee and bread and *praeterea nihil*. That's what we should have had," he pronounced tragically, shaking his head in retrospective consternation at the thing escaped. "Oh, these starveling Continental breakfasts! But I threw myself upon Pia's clemency. I paid her compliments upon her hair, upon her toilet. I called her Pia mia. I said that if I had only met her earlier in life, I should have been a very different person. I appealed to the *woman* in her. I explained to her that my hollow-cheeked companion, with the lack-lustre eye, was a star-crossed lover, and must be treated with exceptional tenderness. I said that nothing mitigated the *tormento d'amore* like beginning the day with a sustaining meal. I said you were a man of an unbounded stomach. I said you were subject to paroxysms of the most violent rage, and if you did n't get the proper variety and quantity of food, you 'd smash the furniture. I smiled upon her with my bonniest, blithest eyne. I ogled her. I chucked her under the chin. I did nothing of the sort. I was extremely dignified. But I told her of a dream I had last night—oh, such a lovely dream—and she was melted. What do you suppose I dreamed of? I dreamed of plump, juicy English sausages."

His face grew wistful, his voice sank. He piled his plate with ham and omelette.

"You 'd better write a song about it," fleered Anthony. "'The Homesick Glutton's Dream.'" Then, making a face, "Why did you order coffee?" he grumbled. "Why did n't you order tea?"

"Tut, don't be peevish," said Adrian. "Sit up, and tie your table-napkin round your neck, and try to be polite when the kind gentleman speaks to you. I did order tea. But tea at Sampaolo is regarded in the light of a pharmaceutical preparation. Pia said she thought I might be able to procure some at the *farmacia*. This omelette really is n't bad. You 'd better take some—before it disappears in the darkness."

But Anthony declined the omelette—and it disappeared in the darkness.

"Come, cheer up, goodman Dull," Adrian exhorted him, selecting the truffled portions from a plateful of gallantine. "'Men have died, and worms have eaten them, but not for love.' Ginger is still hot in the mouth, and there are more fish in the sea than have ever yet nibbled at your bait and spurned it. Do you know why there are no mosquitoes at Sampaolo, and no bandits? There are none—Pia gave me her word for it, Pia mia gave me her pretty feminine word. But do you know why? Pia told me why. The wind, Signore. The wind blows them away—away, away, and far away, over the bright blue sea. Every afternoon we get a wind, sweeping in from the north. Sometimes it is only a *venticello*, sometimes a *temporale*, sometimes an *orogano terribile*, but it is always sufficient to blow away the mosquitoes and the bandits. Pia told me so. Sweet Pia."

"Humph," said Anthony.

"Humph, by all means," Adrian hastened to agree. "I have a sort of humphy feeling myself—a sort of unsatisfied yearning, that is scarcely akin to pain, and resembles sorrow only as the mist resembles the rain. I think it may be imputed to inadequate nourishment. I think I will try some of that mortadella, if you 'll be so good as to pass it. Thank you. And another cup of coffee, with plenty of whipped cream on top, please. How cruel dairymaids must be, to whip such nice stuff as cream. But they 're cruel only to be kind, are n't they?—cruel to the cream, to be kind to us, the dear creatures. If you 'd give up smoking and drinking, you 'd have a healthy appetite yourself. Come! Be comforted. Cast off this green and yellow melancholy. Take me for your exemplar. I too, when I first visited my ancestral home, I too was filled with horror and resentment. I entered it screaming, as I am credibly informed, kicking and screaming, protesting with all the passion of latent genius, with all the force of a brand-new pair of lungs. But I 've enjoyed it very well ever since. Ah, the strange tale of Man. Conceived in sin, brought forth in pain, to live and amuse himself in an impenetrable environment of mystery—in an impenetrable fog. And never to see, of all things, his own face! To see the faces of others, to see the telescopic stars and the microscopic microbes, yet never to see his own face. And even the reflection, the shadow of it, which he can see in a looking-glass, even that he perforce sees *à rebours*. You can't deny it's rum. But if I had a face as long as yours, I solemnly believe, I should deem it likewise providential."

"To think, to think," Anthony, long-faced, was brooding, "that she in mere wilfulness has condemned me to a whole mortal week of this."

"We lunch," said Adrian, "at one, though Pia suggested twelve, and dine at seven, though Pia suggested six. At four we shall have a little *goûté—caffé con pasticceria*—to take the place of tea. And now, if you can tear yourself from the pleasures of the table, let's be up and doing. We 'll begin with the Cathedral, and if we look sharp, we 'll be in time to hear a Mass. There are Masses every half hour till ten. Then the Palazzo Rosso. After luncheon and a brief siesta, Isola Nobile. And after our *caffé con pasticceria*, a donkey-ride in the country."

When they had heard their Mass, they were approached by the Sacristan, a little, shrunken, brown old man in a cassock, who offered to serve them as a guide. The church was very dim and very silent. Here and there a woman knelt at prayer; here and there a candle burned. The Sacristan removed the frontal from the High Altar, to show them the golden reliquary that enshrines the dust of San Guido, and unveiled the three fine altar-pieces, attributed to Giacomo Fiorentino, "San Guido Shipwrecked," "San Guide's Return," and "The Good Death of San Guido." He showed them also, in its glass case, the Sword of the Golden Thorn, reciting its history; and finally he conducted them to the crypt, where, under masses of sculptured ner'-antico, emblazoned with their armorials, some five-and-twenty generations of Valdeschi lie entombed. What were Anthony's emotions? He must have had emotions.

At the Palazzo Rosso they were invited to write their names and nationality in the visitors' book; and then a silver-haired, soft-voiced, gentle-mannered servitor in livery led them up the grand marble staircase and through an endless suite of airy, stately rooms—rooms with floors of polished concrete, displaying elaborate patterns, with tapestried walls and frescoed ceilings, with sparse but ancient and precious articles of furniture, chandeliers of Venetian glass, Venetian mirrors, and innumerable paintings, many of them portraits.

"It's astonishing," said Adrian, "how, by some occult process of selection, in spite of perpetual marriage with new blood, in spite of the thousand vicissitudes of time and circumstance, in a given family a particular feature will persist. There 's the Habsburg lip, for instance. And here is the Valdeschi nose. From generation to generation, from century to century, one can recognize in these dead forefathers of yours the identical nose that is on your face to-day."

It was quite true. Again and again you saw repeated the same high-bridged, slenderly aquiline nose.

"Sala del trono," announced their cicerone (only, he pronounced it *Sa' do truno*).

And there, sure enough, at the end of a vast chamber, was "the great scarlet throne, with the gilded coronet topping the canopy above," just as Susanna had described it. What were Anthony's emotions?

But the white-haired serving-man (as Adrian noticed) from time to time allowed his eyes to fix themselves studiously upon Anthony's face, and appeared to fall into a muse. Now he stopped before a high white-and-gold double-door. "The entrance to the private apartments," he said, and placed his hand upon the fancifully-wrought ormolu door-knob.

"Are the public admitted to the private apartments," Anthony doubted, holding back.

"No, Signore," said the old man. "But I think, if the Signore will pardon me, that the Signore's Excellency will be a connection of the family."

Anthony all but jumped.

"Why on earth should you think that?" he wondered.

"It's the persistent feature," said Adrian, in English, with a chuckle. "The Signore's Excellency is betrayed by the Signore's Excellency's beak."

"If the Signore will pardon me, I observed that the Signore's name, when he wrote in the visitors' book, was Crahforrdi of England," the old man explained. "But the Crahforrdi of England are a house cognate to ours. The consort of the Conte who was Conte when I had the honour of entering the family, nearly sixty years ago, was a Crahforrdi of England, a lordessa. Moreover it is in the Signore's face. If the Signori will favour me, it will give me great pleasure to show them what they will think is the Signore's own portrait."

In size and shape the private apartments were simply a continuation of the state apartments, but they were furnished in modern fashion, with a great deal of luxury, and, in so far as the enveloping brown hollands would permit one to opine, with a great deal of taste. "The family occupy this palace during the cold months only. In summer they make a villeggiatura to Isola Nobile. Therefore you do not see these rooms at their best," the old man apologized. In what he described as the *gabine'o segre'o* of the Countess, over the fireplace, hung the full-length, life-size portrait of a gentleman, in the dress of eighteen-forty-something—high stock, flowered waistcoat, close-fitting buff trousers, and full-bottomed blue frock-coat, very tight above the hips.

"Count Antonio the Seventeenth, the last of our tyrants. The Signori will be aware that we were tyrants of Sampaolo for many centuries," said the old man, not without a touch of pride. Then, bowing to Anthony, "One would think properly the portrait of your Excellency."

Indeed, the face of the last of the tyrants and his grandson's face were surprisingly alike.

"Conte Antonio Decimose'mo was Conte when, as a lad, I had the honour to join the family," the old servant went on. "It was he who had for consort the Lordessa Crahforrdi of England. After his death, there was the Revolution, by which we annexed to Sampaolo another island called Sardinia. The Lordessa was taken prisoner in these rooms, with the Conte-figlio, and banished from the country. Then the King of Sardinia was elected tyrant of both islands, and the government was removed from Vallanza to Turin. That was many years ago, fifty years ago. When the Pope died, the government was again removed, and now it is at Rome."

"Oh? Is the Pope dead?" Adrian questioned.

"Che sì, Signore—dupo lung' anni," the old man assured him.

They strolled about the town for a little, before returning to the hotel— through the narrow cobble-paved streets, with their alternations of splendour and squalor, their palaces, churches, hovels, their dark little shops, their neglected shrines, their vociferous population, their heterogeneous smells—and along the Riva, with its waterside bustle, its ships loading and unloading, and its unexampled view of bay and mountains.

"Do you see this stick?" asked Adrian, holding up his walking-stick.

"What about it?" asked Anthony.

"I 'm coming to that," said Adrian. "But first you must truthfully answer a question. Which end of this stick would you prefer to be—the bright silver handle or the earth-stained ferrule?"

"Don't know," said Anthony, with an air of weariness.

"Don't you?" marvelled Adrian. "How funny. Well, then, you must understand that this stick is but an emblem—a thing's sign. Now for the thing signified. Have you ever paused to moralize over the irony that determines the fates of families? Take, for example, a family that begins with a great man—a great soldier, a great saint, for instance—and then for evermore thereafter produces none but mediocrities. I hope you perceive the irony of that. But contrariwise, take a family that goes on for centuries producing mediocrities, and suddenly ends with the production of a genius.

Take my family, just for a case in point. Here I come of a chain of progenitors reaching straight back to Adam; and of not one of them save Adam and myself, has the world ever heard. And even Adam owes his celebrity not in the least to his personal endowments, but solely to the unique character of his position. The First Man could n't help getting a certain reputation, would he, n'ould he. But from Adam to Adrian—silence. Then sudden silvery music. And Adrian—mark the predestination—Adrian is childless. He is the last link. With him the chain, five thousand years long, stops. He is the sudden brilliant flare-up of the fire before it goes out. Well, now, tell me—which end of this stick would you prefer to be? The shining silver handle, or the dull iron other end?"

They were conveyed to Isola Nobile in one of those long slender Sampaolese *vipere*—boats that are a good deal like gondolas, except that they have no felze, and carry a short mast at the bow, with a sail that is only spread when the wind is directly aft. I suppose the palace at Isola Nobile is one of the most beautiful in the world, with its four mellow-toned marble façades rising sheer out of the water, with its long colonnades, its graceful moresque windows, and the variety, profusion, and lace-like delicacy of its carved and incised details. Here again they had to write their names in the visitors' book, and again a servant (this time a young and rather taciturn person) led them through countless vast and splendid rooms, far more splendid than those at the Palazzo Rosso, rooms rich with porphyry, alabaster, mosaics, gilded flourishes and arabesques of stucco, and containing many treasures of painting and sculpture, some of which, I believe, even the sceptical Morellists allow to be actually the handiwork of the artists to whom they are ascribed. But so far from there being any question of their visiting the private apartments at Isola Nobile, their guide, at one point in their progress, sprang forward and hurriedly closed a door that had stood open, and through which they had caught a glimpse of a pleasantly furnished library. By and by they were passed on to a gardener, who showed them the gardens on Isola Fratello and Isola Sorella, with their camphor-trees and cedars, their oranges, oleanders, magnolias, laurels, their terraces, whence thousands of lizards whisked away at the approach of Man, their fountains, grottoes, temples, their peacocks, flamingoes, and tame ring-doves, and always, always, with that wonderful outlook upon the bay and its girdle of sun-bathed hills. The gardener plucked many flowers for them, so that they returned to Vallanza with armfuls of roses, lilies, oleanders, and jessamine.

Later that afternoon, Adrian having gone alone for his donkey-ride in the country (more power to the back of the donkey!), Anthony was seated by the open window of his bedroom, in a state of deep depression. All at once, between the two promontories that form the entrance to the bay, the

Capo del Papa and the Capo del Turco, appeared, heading for Vallanza, a white steamer, clearly, from its size and lines, a yacht—a very bright and gay object to look upon, as it gleamed in the sun and crisped the blue waters. And all at once, his eye automatically following it, Anthony experienced a perfectly inexplicable lightening of the heart,—as if, indeed, the white yacht were bringing something good to him. It was absurd, but he could not help it. Somehow, his depression left him, and a feeling almost of joyousness took its place.

"She said she loved me—she said she loved me," he remembered. "And at the farthest," he reflected, "at the farthest I shall be with her again in nine little days."

He got out the fan that he had stolen, and pressed it to his face. He got out his writing-materials, and wrote her a long, cheerful, impassioned letter.

His change of mood was all the more noteworthy, perhaps, because the yacht chanced to be the *Fiorimondo*, bearing the Countess of Sampaolo and her suite from Venice, whither it had proceeded two days before, upon orders telegraphed from Paris.

XXI

Adrian, coming in, saw Anthony's letter, superscribed and stamped, lying on the table.

"I 'm posting a lot of stuff of my own," he said. "Shall I post this with it?"

Had Susanna admitted him to her confidence? How otherwise could it have befallen, as it did, that she received Anthony's letter, which was of course addressed to Craford, at Isola Nobile no later than that very evening?

She read it, smiling.

"Which of the many villas that overlook the bay and are visible from my window, with their white walls and dark-green gardens,—which is yours?" he questioned. "All day I have been wondering. That is the single thing that really stirs me here, that really gives me a *feeling*—its association with you. All day I have been hearing a sonnet of Ronsard's—do you remember it?— *Voicy le bois*. But I wish I knew which villa is your villa, which garden is your garden. Why did n't I find out before I was driven from Paradise? I could easily find out here by inquiring, I suppose. But your name is too sacred. I can't profane it by speaking it aloud to people who might not bare their heads at the sound of it."

Susanna tittered.

And on another page (the letter was eight pages long) he said:—

"It is all very beautiful, of course,—the way the town piles itself up against the hillside, the pink and yellow and lilac *blondeur* of the houses, the olive gardens, the radiant sky overhead,—it is all very picturesque and beautiful. But I am not hungry for beauty—at least, for this beauty. If you were here with me,—ah, then indeed! But you are not here, and I am hungry for Craford. There was a time when Craford used to seem to me the tritest spot in Europe, and the thought of Italy was luminous of everything romantic, of everything to be desired. There was a time when nothing gave me such joy as to wake and remember, 'I am in Italy—in Italy—in Italy!'— in Rome or Florence or Venice, as the case might be. But the times have changed, have changed. *You* were in Italy in those days, and now you are at Craford. Italy is dust and ashes. I hunger for Craford as the only place in the world where life is life."

And on still another page:—

"I can't deny that I got a certain emotion in the grey old Cathedral. For so many generations one's people were baptized there, married there, buried there. And then how many times must *you* have worshipped there, heard holy Mass there. They showed us the relics of San Guido and the Spina d'Oro, of course, and—well, one is n't made of wood. I tried to make up my mind in what part of the church you usually knelt, which prie-dieu was your prie-dieu,—I 'm afraid without any very notable success. But one felt something like a faint afterglow of your presence, and it made one's heart beat. Again at the Palazzo Rosso, under the eyes of all those motionless and silent, dead and gone Valdeschi, in their armour, in their ruffs and puffs and periwigs, one could n't be entirely wooden. The servant who showed us about, an old man who said he had been in the family for I forget how many hundred years, hailed me as a 'cognate,' having recognized the name of Craford, and thereupon inducted us into the *appartamenti segreti*, to exhibit a portrait of my grandsire. Wood itself, I dare say, must have vibrated a little at that. In the throne-room I was suddenly caught up and whisked away, back to a rainy afternoon at Craford; and I walked beside you on the cliffs, and heard your voice, and rejoiced in the sense of your nearness to me, and in your adorable beauty, as you breasted the wind, with the sea and the sky for a background. (Do you remember? Do you remember how keen and sweet the air was, with the scent of the wild thyme? and how the sand-martins circled round us?) As we passed through the long, bare, imposing rooms, something like a shadow of you seemed to flit before us. Or if I glanced out of one of the tall windows, it seemed as if you had just passed under them, along the Riva or across the Piazza. As for Isola Nobile, if I regret that it is n't mine, that is chiefly because I should be glad to be in a position to offer so very lordly and lovely a pleasure-house to *you*."

Susanna laughed.

Towards the end he wrote:—

"I look at the sea and I realize that it is continuous from here to England, from here to Rowland Marshes; and it seems somehow to connect us, to keep us in touch. Perhaps you, too, are looking at it at this same moment. I fancy you walking on your terrace, and looking off upon the grey-blue sea. It seems somehow to connect us. But there is no grey in the blue of the sea here—it is blue, blue, unmitigated, almost dazzling blue, save where in the sun it turns to quite dazzling white, or in the deeper shadows takes on tints that are almost crimson, tints of *lie-de-vin*. Oh, why are n't you here? If you were here, I think a veil would fall from before my eyes, and I should see everything differently. I could imagine myself *loving* Sampaolo—if you were here. In nine days—nine days! And to-morrow it will be only eight days, and the day after to-morrow only seven. *Only* do I say? I count in that fashion to keep my courage up. Nine days! Why can't those nine eternities be annihilated from the calendar? Why does n't some kind person kill me, and then call me back to life in nine days? Oh, it was cruel of you, cruel, cruel."

Susanna looked out of her window, across the dark bay, to where the electric lamps along the Riva threw wavering fronds of light upon the water. She kissed her hand, and wafted the kiss (as nearly as the darkness would let her guess) in the direction of the Piazza San Guido. Then she went into the library, and hunted for a volume of Ronsard.

XXII

There are two men, as they that know Sampaolo will not need to be reminded, two young men, who, during the summer months, pervade the island. In winter they go to Rome, or to Nice, or to England for the hunting; but in summer they pervade Sampaolo, where they have a villa just outside Vallanza, as well as the dark old palace of their family in the town.

The twin brothers, Franco and Baldo del Ponte—who that has once met them can ever forget them? To begin with, they are giants—six-feet-four, and stalwart in proportion. Then they are handsome giants, with good, strong, regular features, close-cropped brown hair that tends to curl, and hearty open-air complexions. Then they are jolly, pleasant-tempered, simple-minded and clean-minded giants. Then they are indefatigable giants—indefatigable in the pursuit of open-air amusements: now in their sailing-boats, now in their motor-cars, or on horse-back, or driving their four-in-hands. And finally, being Italians, they are Anglophile giants;—like so many of the Italian aristocracy, they are more English than the English. They are rigorously English in their dress, for instance; they have all their clothes from London, and these invariably of the latest mode. They give English names to their sailing-boats—the *Mermaid*, the *Seagull.* They employ none but Englishmen in their stables, which are of English design, with English fittings. They have English dogs,—fox-terriers, bull-terriers, collies,—also with English names, Toby, Jack, Spark, Snap, and so forth. They speak English with only the remotest trace of foreignness—were they not educated at Eton, and at Trinity College, Cambridge? And they would fain Anglicise, not merely the uniform of the Italian police, but the Italian constitution. "What Italy needs," they will assure you, looking wondrous wise, "is a House of Peers." Their Italian friends laugh at them a good deal; but I suspect that under the laughter there is a certain admiration, if not even (for, as Italian fortunes go, theirs is an immense one) a certain envy.

Is all this apropos of boots, you wonder? No, for behold—

After breakfast, on the following morning, Adrian was alone, enjoying a meditative digestion, in the sitting-room at the Hôtel de Rome, when he saw come bowling along the Riva, turn rattling into the Piazza, and draw up at the inn door, a very English-looking dog-cart, driven by a huge young man in tweeds, with an apparent replica of himself beside him, and an English-looking groom behind. The two huge young men descended; he who had driven said something inaudible to the groom; and the groom, touching his hat, answered: "Yes, my lord."

"So," thought Adrian, "we are not the only Britons in this island. I wonder who my lord is."

And then, nothing if not consequent, he began to sing, softly to himself—

"Lord of thy presence, and no land besi-i-ide . . ."

And he was still softly carolling that refrain, when the door of the sitting-room was opened.

"Marchese del Ponte, Marchese Baldo del Ponte," announced the waiter, with sympathetic exhilaration, flourishing his inseparable napkin.

The two huge young men entered. The room seemed all at once to contract, and become half its former size.

"Ah, Count," said one of them, advancing, and getting hold of Adrian's hand. "How do you do? I am the Marchese del Ponte; this is my brother, the Marchese Baldo. Welcome to Sampaolo. We are your connections, you know. Our ancestors have intermarried any time these thousand years."

Adrian's rosy face was wreathed in his most amiable smiles.

"How do you do? I 'm very glad to see you. Won't you take chairs?" he responded, and hospitably pushed chairs forward. "But I 'm afraid," he added, shaking his head, still smiling, "I 'm afraid I 'm not a count."

"Ah, yes," said Baldo, "we know you don't use your title."

"You 're a count all right, whether you use your title or not," said Franco. "Noblesse is in the bone. You can't get rid of it."

"Your great-grandmother was a Ponte," said Baldo, "and our own grandmother was a Valdeschi, your grandfather's cousin."

"Really?" said Adrian, pleasantly. "But I 'm afraid," he explained to Franco, "that there is n't any noblesse in *my* bones. I 'm afraid I 'm just a plain commoner."

"Oh, you refer to the Act of Proscription—I understand," said Franco. "But that was utterly invalid—a mere piece of political stage-play. The Italian government had no more power to proscribe your title than it would have to proscribe an English peerage,—no jurisdiction. It could create a new Count of Sampaolo, which it did; but it could n't abolish the dignity of the existing Count—a dignity that was ancient centuries before the Italian government was dreamed of. You 're a count all right."

"I see," said Adrian. "And are you, then," he inferred, with sprightly interest, "agin the government?"

The familiar formula appeared to tickle the two young Anglophiles inordinately. They greeted it with deep-chested laughter.

"We 're not exactly *agin* the government," Baldo answered, "but we believe in remodelling it. What Italy needs"—he looked a very Solon; and his brother nodded concurrence in his opinion——"is a House of Lords."

"I see—I see," said Adrian.

"We want you to come and stay with us," said Franco. "We 've a villa half a mile up the Riva. You 'd be more comfortable there than here, and it would give us the greatest pleasure to have you."

"The greatest possible pleasure," cordially echoed Baldo.

"You 're exceedingly good," said Adrian. "And I should be most happy. But I 'm afraid—"

"Not another word," protested Franco. "You 'll come. That' s settled."

"That's settled," echoed Baldo.

"We 'll send down for your traps this afternoon," said Franco. "Have you a man with you? No? Then we 'll send Grimes. He 'll pack for you, and bring up your traps. But we hope to carry you off with us now—in time for luncheon."

"I don't know how to thank you," said Adrian. "But I 'm afraid—I hate to destroy an illusion, yet in honesty I must—I 'm afraid I 'm not the person you take me for. I 'm afraid there's a misapprehension. I—"

"Oh, we 'll respect your incog all right, if that's what's troubling you," promised Baldo. "You shall be Mr. Anthony Craford."

"Craford *of* Craford," Franco corrected him.

"But there it is," said Adrian. "Now see how I 'm forced to disappoint you. I 'm awfully sorry, but I 'm *not* Mr. Anthony Craford—no, nor Craford *of* Craford, either."

"What?" puzzled Franco.

"Not Craford?" puzzled Baldo.

"No," said Adrian, sadly. "I 'm awfully sorry, but my name is Willes."

"Willes?" said Franco. "But it was Craford in the visitors' book at the Palazzo Rosso. That's how we knew you were here."

"My brother is the Hereditary Constable of the Palace," said Baldo. "It is now merely an honorary office. But the visitors' book is brought to him whenever there have been any visitors."

"And we inquired for Craford downstairs," supplemented Franco. "And they said you were at home, and showed us up."

"I 'm awfully sorry," repeated Adrian. "But Craford and I are as distinct as night and morning. Craford has gone out for a solitary walk. My name is Willes. Craford and I are travelling together."

"Oh, I see," cried Franco; and slapping his thigh, "Ho, ho, ho," he laughed.

"Ho, ho, ho," laughed Baldo. "We were jolly well sold."

"We—ho, ho—we got the wrong sow by the ear," laughed Franco.

"We put the saddle on the wrong horse—ho, ho," laughed Baldo.

"We 're delighted to make your acquaintance, all the same," said Franco.

"And we hold you to your promise—you 're to come and stay with us— you and Craford both," said Baldo.

"Yes—there 's no getting out of that. We count upon you," said Franco.

"So far as I 'm concerned, I should be charmed," said Adrian. "But I can't speak for Craford. He 's a bit run down and out of sorts. I 'm not sure whether he 'll feel that he 's in a proper state for paying visits. But here he comes."

He inclined his head towards a window, through which Anthony could be seen crossing the Piazza.

"By Jove!" exclaimed Franco. "I should have known him for a Valdeschi anywhere. He 's exactly like a portrait of his grandfather in the Palazzo Rosso."

"By Jove, so he is," exclaimed Baldo.

And, to Adrian's surprise, when the introductions were accomplished, and the invitation was repeated to him, Anthony at once accepted.

"I 've given orders for my four-in-hand to come round here and pick us up," said Franco. "Shall we all go for a spin, and get an appetite for luncheon?"

"In the afternoon, if there 's a breeze, I propose a sail," said Baldo. "I 've just got a new boat out from England, schooner-rigged, the *Spindrift*. I 've not yet really had a fair chance to try her."

"Do you go in for tennis?" asked Franco. "We 've got a court at the villa."

"I don't know whether you care for swimming," said Baldo. "You get a fairly decent dive-off from the landing-stage at the end of our garden. The water here is pooty good. My brother and I generally go for a swim before dinner."

"Ah, here 's Tom with the four-in-hand," said Franco. And then, with a readiness for self-effacement that was surely less British than the language in which it found expression, "Would you care to take the ribbons, Count?" he asked. And when Anthony had declined, "Would you, Willes?" he proceeded.

"Not just at the start, thanks," said Adrian. "I should like to watch 'em step a bit first."

The hypocrite. As if he would have known what to do with the ribbons, had they been given to him.

So Franco took them himself, while Baldo blew the horn.

"Have you visited Castel San Guido yet?" Franco questioned. "Shall we make that our objective?"

They drove up and up, round and round the winding road that leads to Castel San Guido, where it clings to the almost vertical mountainside. For the greater part the road was bordered by olive orchards, but sometimes there were vineyards, sometimes groves of walnut-trees, clumps of stone-pines, or fields of yellowing maize, and everywhere there were oleanders growing wild, and always there was the view.

Castel San Guido is very like a hundred other mediaeval castles, a grim old fortress, with walls of I forget what prodigious thickness, with round towers pierced by sinister-looking meutrières, and crowned by battlements, with bare stone courts, stone halls, cold and dimly lighted, and a dismantled stone chapel. But I dare say the descendant of San Guido (not being made of wood) had his emotions. And the view was magnificent—Vallanza below, its red roofs burning in the sun, the purple bay, the olive-mantled hills, with a haze of gold-dust and pearl-dust brooding over them, and white-walled villages shining in twenty improbable situations, with their dark cypresses and slender campanili.

They had toiled up slowly, but they came spinning back at a tremendous pace, down the steep gradients, round the perilous curves, while Franco, his jaws shut tight, his brows drawn together, gave all his attention to his horses, Baldo merrily wound his horn, Anthony smoked cigarettes, and Adrian, for dear life, with his heart in his mouth, held hard to the seat-rail at his side. I think he pushed a very genuine *ouf*, when, without accident, they had regained the level ground.

The Villa del Ponte is a long grey rectangular building, as severe in outward aspect as a barrack or a prison, in a garden that stretches right away to the sea-wall, a garden full of palms, oranges, tall, feathery eucalyptus-trees, and lizards, perfectly Italian. But no sooner do you pass the portal of the house, than you leave Italy, as on a magic-carpet, and find yourself in the seventh circle of England, amid English furniture, English books, English periodicals, daily, weekly, monthly, (the *Pink 'un* perhaps the most conspicuous), and between walls embellished by English sporting-pictures and the masks and brushes of English foxes. "We hunt a good bit, you know," said Franco. "We've a little box in Northamptonshire, and hunt with the Pytchley. We both have the button." One was n't in the least surprised when an English voice, proceeding from the smuggest of smooth-shaven English countenances, informed my lord that luncheon was served.

After luncheon they sailed in the *Spindrift*. After that, (to Adrian's delight, I hope) they had tea, with plenty of buttered toast. Then they played tennis. Then they went for a breathless whirl along the Riva in a motor-car. Then they swam. And after dinner they played billiards, while Franco and Baldo smoked short pipes, and sipped whiskey and soda—but a half-pennyworth of whiskey, as Adrian noticed, to an intolerable deal of soda. Blood will tell, and theirs, in spite of everything, was abstemious Italian blood.

XXIII

"Now, Commendatore," said Susanna, making her face grave, "listen, and you shall hear"—but then her gravity broke down—"of the midnight ride of Paul Revere," she concluded, laughing.

She raised her eyes to his, aglow with that tender, appealing, mocking, defiant smile of hers. He, poor man, smiled too, though not very happily, I fear—nay, even with a kind of suspicious bewilderment, as one who sniffs brewing mischief, but knows not of what particular variety it will be. They were seated in the shade and the coolness of a long open colonnade at Isola Nobile, while, all round them, the August morning, like a thing alive, pulsated with warmth and light, and the dancing waves of the bay lapped musically against the walls below. The Commendatore was clad in stiffly-starched white duck, and held a white yachting-cap in his hand. Susanna wore a costume of some cool gauzy tissue, pearl-grey, with white ruffles that looked as impalpable as froth.

"Listen," she said, "and you shall hear of the midday quest of Commendatore Fregi. I will tell you step by step what steps you are to take. My cousin is staying with the Ponte brothers at their villa. Well,—first step of all,—you are to call upon him."

"No," said the Commendatore, jerking his head, his baldish old head with its fringe of iron-grey curls.

"Yes," said Susanna, resolutely compressing her lips.

"No," said he. "It is not etiquette. The new-comer pays the first call."

"That is Italian etiquette," said she. "But my cousin is an Englishman."

"*Nun fa nien'e.* He is in Italy. He must conform to the customs of the country," insisted Commendatore Fregi, in the dialect of Sampaolo, twirling his fierce old moustaches, glaring with his mild old eyes.

"No," said Susanna, softly, firmly; "we must stretch a point in his favour. He is English. We will adopt the custom of *his* country. So you will call upon him. I wish it."

"Ph-h-h," puffed the Commendatore, fanning himself with his cap. "Well—?" he questioned.

Susanna, in her diaphanous light-coloured frock, leaned back, smiling. The Commendatore fanned himself rapidly with his cap, and waited for her instructions.

"You call upon him, you introduce yourself as an old friend of the family. 'As a boy, I knew your grandfather, your grandmother, and I was a playfellow of your father's.'"

She threw back her head, pouted out her lips, and achieved a very admirable counterfeit of the Commendatore's manner.

"You ask the usual questions, pay the usual compliments. 'Can I have the pleasure of serving you in anyway? I beg leave to place myself at your disposal. You must not fail to command me'—and patati and patata."

"You are an outrageous little ape," said the Commendatore, grinning in spite of himself. "You would mimic the Devil to his face."

"No," said Susanna. "I only mimic people when I am fond of them."

And again she lifted her eyes to his, where they melted in her tender, teasing smile.

"Ph-h-h," puffed the Commendatore, agitating his cap.

"And then," pursued Susanna, "having paid the usual compliments, you rise to go."

"Ah—*bene*," said the Commendatore, and his lean old yellow face looked a good deal relieved.

"Yes," said she. "But then, having risen to go, then, like the wily and supple diplomat you are, you come to the real business of your visit."

"Oh?" said the Commendatore.

He sat forward, on the edge of his chair, and frowned. He had thought his troubles were over, and now it appeared that they had not yet begun.

"Yes," said Susanna. "Having risen to go, you pause, you hesitate, and then suddenly you take your courage in both hands. 'Count,' you say, 'I wish to speak to you about your cousin.' And thereupon, frankly, confidentially, you proceed to lay before him the difficulties of your position. 'I was your cousin's guardian; I am still her nearest friend; I occupy the place of a parent towards her, and feel myself responsible for her. And one of my chief concerns, one of my first duties, is, of course, to see that she makes a good marriage. She is a great heiress—she would be the natural prey of fortune-hunters. I must protect her, I must direct her. With one hand I must keep away undesirable suitors, with the other hand I must catch a desirable one. But now observe my perplexities. Your cousin is peculiar.

She is not in the least like the typical submissive young Italian girl. She is excessively self-willed, capricious, fantastic, unreasonable——'"

"Bravo," put in the Commendatore, clapping his bony old hands. "I can say all that with a clear conscience." He twirled his moustaches again.

"Do you think I would ask you to say anything you could n't say with a clear conscience?" Susanna demanded, with a glance of reproach. "So, with a clear conscience, you go on: 'Your cousin is fantastic, unreasonable, sentimental, romantic, extravagant. And—to come to the point—she has got it into her unreasonable and romantic little head that she has no right to the position which she occupies. She has studied the history of her family, and she has got it into her perverse little head that by the changes which took place in 1850 a very great injustice was perpetrated. She has persuaded herself, in short, that the properties here at Sampaolo, which are technically and legally hers, are rightfully and morally *yours*; and, to tell you the whole truth, since my guardianship expired, a few months ago, I have had hard work to restrain her from taking measures to relinquish those properties in your favour.' No—don't interrupt," she forbade him, when the Commendatore made as if to speak.

A sound of guttural impatience died in the old man's throat. He fanned himself nervously, while Susanna, smiling, resumed the lesson.

"'But,' you declare with energy, 'I *have* restrained her, and I shall continue to restrain her. She could only make the properties over to you by becoming a nun and taking vows of perpetual poverty. I will fight to my dying gasp to prevent her from doing that. However'—and now you change your note, and speak as one anxious to conciliate and convince—'however, it has occurred to me that there is a simple course by which the whole awkward situation could be solved—by which your cousin's scruples could be set at rest, and you yourself put in possession of your ancestral estates. My dear Count, your cousin is a charming girl, and it is my chief concern and duty to arrange a suitable marriage for her. Let me have the very great satisfaction of arranging a marriage between her and you.'"

Susanna leaned back, and laughed. But the Commendatore frowned at her with genuine anger.

"*Macché!*" he cried. "What fool's talk is this? What farce are you preparing?"

"No farce," said Susanna, gently. "Only a wedding—at which you shall give the bride away. And now—the launch is waiting. The sooner you are off, the sooner you 'll return."

"Never," said the Commendatore. "I would sell myself to be chopped into sausage-meat, before I would become a party to any such carnival tricks."

"Carnival tricks? Do you call marriage a carnival trick?" Susanna wondered. "Or do you wish me to live and die an old maid? Is it or is it not your duty to arrange a suitable match for me?"

"It is not my duty to arrange a match for you with a foreigner whom I have n't the honour of knowing," he retorted.

"Well, then," urged Susanna, "go to my cousin and make him the proposition I have suggested. And if he says yes,—if he consents to marry me,—I give you my most solemn promise that not for any consideration in the world will I accept him."

"What?" questioned the Commendatore, blinking at her.

"If he says yes, I 'll say no. If he says no, he says no. So it is no, either way," she pointed out. "And meanwhile—the launch is waiting."

"If he says no!" scoffed the Commendatore. "Is the man born who will say no to a bag of gold?"

"That's exactly what you have now an opportunity of discovering," she replied. "But if he says yes, I give you my solemn promise, it will be the end of him, so far as I 'm concerned."

The Commendatore rubbed the back of his neck.

"I never heard such a gallimaufry of headless and tailless nonsense," he declared.

"Think of that poor long-suffering launch," said Susanna. "You are still keeping it waiting."

"It may wait till the sea dries up, for all of me," said the Commendatore, settling himself in his seat. "Do you take me for Pulcinella? I will not begin at my time of life to play carnival tricks."

"Ah, well, after all," said Susanna, "it does n't really matter very much."

And apparently she abandoned her intention. But after a pause she added, rather as if speaking to herself, "I must send for Father Angelo, I suppose."

"*What?*" snapped out the Commendatore, sitting up.

"Yes," said Susanna, dreamily, "Father Angelo. *He* won't refuse to do what I ask him to."

"Bah," said the Commendatore. "A priest—a monk—a shaveling—a bare-toes."

"A very good, kind, holy man," said Susanna. "And as my cousin is a faithful Catholic, I think on all accounts Father Angelo will serve my purpose best."

"Peuh—a Jesuit," said the Commendatore, elevating his nose.

"He is n't a Jesuit—he is a Capuchin," said Susanna.

"They are all Jesuits," said the Commendatore, with a sweeping gesture. "A brown-back—a funeral-follower—a prayer-monger," he growled, brushing his immense moustaches upwards, to emphasize his scorn.

"Hush," Susanna remonstrated, lifting her hand. "You must n't rail against religion."

"I do not rail against religion," answered the Commendatore. "Taken in moderation, religion is an excellent thing—for women. Did I not see that you were religiously brought up? But when it comes to these priests, these Jesuits,—when it comes to that Father Angelo,—I would have them all hung up and smoke-dried, to make bacon of. Garrh!" he snorted, tossing his head.

"Yes, I know," murmured Susanna. "You were always jealous of Father Angelo."

"I? Jealous of that gnawer of fish-bones? It is probable," sniffed the Commendatore.

He rose from his chair, and stood before her, very slim and erect, his chin thrust forward, so that the tendons of his long thin neck showed like wires.

"But I am an old ass. I can deny you nothing. I go to your cousin," he consented.

"You are an old dear," said Susanna. "I knew you would go."

Her eyes were brimming with mirth, with triumph, with fondness. She rose too, and gently patted his stiffly-starched white duck sleeve.

After he was gone, she crossed one of the light marble bridges, and walked in the garden on Isola Sorella, where it was shaded by a row of ilexes. Blackcaps (those tireless ubiquitous minstrels) were singing wildly overhead; ring-doves kept up their monotonous coo-cooing. Beyond, in the sun, butterflies flitted among the flowers, cockchafers heavily droned and blundered, a white peacock strutted, and at the water's edge two long-legged, wry-necked flamingoes stood motionless, like sentinels. At the other side of the ilexes stretched a bit of bright green lawn, with a fountain plashing in the middle, from whose spray the sun struck sparks of iridescent fire; and then, terrace upon terrace, the garden rose to a summit, where there was a belvedere.

I don't know how many times Susanna strolled backwards and forwards, I don't know how many times she looked at her watch. Here and there semi-circular marble benches were placed. Sometimes she would sit down and rest for a little; but she was soon up again, walking, walking, looking at her watch. At last she left the shade, crossed the lawn, ascended the terraces, between orange and lemon-trees with their undergrowth of jessamine, and entered the belvedere, having by this progress created a panic indescribable in the community of lizards.

From the belvedere she could command the whole sunlit surface of the bay, here blue, here silver, here deepening to violet, paling to green, here dimly, obscurely rose. A fleet of fishing-boats, their coloured sails decorated with stripes and geometric patterns, or even now and then with a representation of the owner's patron-saint, was putting out to sea in single file, between the Capo del Turco and the Capo del Papa. But Susanna concentrated her attention upon a part of the shore, perhaps half a mile distant, and half a mile to the east of Vallanza, where the grey-green of the prevailing olives was broken by the dark-green of a garden. The garden ran out into the bay a little, forming a point. Susanna waited and watched, watched and waited, till, by-and-by, from behind the point, a boat appeared, a launch, and came swiftly bobbing over the waves towards Isola Nobile. She must have kept very still during this vigil, for now, when she turned to leave the belvedere, she saw that at least a hundred lizards had come forth from their hiding-places, and were staring at her with their twinkling little pin-heads of eyes. But even as she saw them—zrrrp!—a flash, a rustle, and there was not a lizard anywhere in sight.

She went back to the colonnade.

"My dear," said Commendatore Fregi, "your cousin is an extremely fine fellow, and upon my word I am sorry that my mission to him has failed. I could not hope to find you a better husband."

Whatever the Commendatore's emotion might be, it generally impelled him to do something to his moustaches. Now he pulled them straight out at either side.

"Your mission has failed?" asked Susanna. "How do you mean?"

"He cannot marry you," said the Commendatore, with a shake of the head, a shrug of the shoulders. "He is engaged to a lady in England."

"Ah—I see," said Susanna.

"He is very good-looking," said the Commendatore. "He is his grandfather come back to life."

"Is he indeed?" said Susanna.

"Yes," affirmed the Commendatore. "He dresses well. He has a good manner. He is very quiet."

"Englishmen are apt to be quiet," said Susanna.

"He speaks Italian as well as I do," went on the Commendatore. "But he cannot speak Sampaolese."

"He could easily learn Sampaolese," said Susanna.

"Yes," said the Commendatore. "When I repeated that humbug about your becoming a nun and resigning the properties to him, he held up his hands in horror. 'She must not think of such a thing,' he cried. 'Tell the young lady that I could never conceivably accept such a sacrifice. I understand her scruples, and they do her great honour. But she and I and all of us must accept the situation as we find it. She must not think of becoming a nun.' You see, he has good sense as well as good feeling. That is what I have always told you myself—we must accept the situation as we find it. There's no use trying to open up the past."

"H'm," said Susanna, on a key of doubt.

"And then, with my heart in the business, for I had seen that he was of the right stuff, then I proposed a marriage," said the Commendatore. "I put it to him as strongly as I could. I painted the advantages in vivid colours. But it was no good. He cannot marry you. He is already betrothed."

"So you said," Susanna reminded him. "To a lady in England, I think?"

"Yes," assented the Commendatore. "It is a pity on our account that he will not throw her over. But it is to his credit. Let me tell you it is not every man in his position who would stick at the point of honour. Consider the alternative. He throws over his Englishwoman, and he becomes master not only of one of the noblest estates in Europe, but of an estate which must have for him the incalculable additional value of being his patrimony." Never chary of gesture, the speaker was at this point lavish of it.

"May I be permitted," said Susanna, raising her eyebrows, "to admire the light-hearted way in which you leave *me* out of the saga?"

"You?" puzzled the Commendatore. "Out of the—what? What is a saga?"

"A Scandinavian legend," Susanna instructed him. "Now see how you leave me out of your Scandinavian legend. 'Consider the alternative,' said you. 'He throws over his Englishwoman, and he becomes—' Well, *you* said, 'Master of a noble estate.' But a really gallant person might have said, 'Husband of a perfectly entrancing Italian woman.'"

She pulled a little face.

"Ha," laughed the Commendatore, briefly. "You must have your joke." And his hand instinctively made for his moustaches. "Well, I am sorry. I can never hope to find you a better husband."

"You need never try," said Susanna. "He will do."

"What?" said the Commendatore.

"He will do," said she. "We'll have a grand wedding in the Cathedral. The Bishop shall officiate, in his very best cope and mitre, and you, with your grandest flourish, shall give the bride away."

The Commendatore shrugged his shoulders, and gazed for commiseration at the sky.

"You are incomprehensible," he said. "Haven't I spent an hour telling you he is affianced to a lady in England?"

"No," said Susanna; "only something like ten minutes."

"Brrr," said the Commendatore, contemptuous of the quibble.

"And anyhow, I shall marry him," said Susanna. "You have made me quite fall in love with him, by your glowing description—and I rather liked him before. The lady in England is neither here nor there. We'll be married in the Cathedral, where so many generations of our ancestors have been married. His friend Mr. Willes shall be best man; and the Pontes shall pontificate in their most British manner, with wedding-favours sent out from London. And so the ancient legitimate line of the Valdeschi shall be restored."

"You are mad," said the Commendatore, simply.

"And you shall offer us a wedding-breakfast at the Villa Fregi," she pursued. "We'll have all sorts of nice things to eat and drink, and you shall propose the health of the bride, and make a magnificent speech. And I shall wear my coronet—which I have never yet worn—for then I shall be the Countess of Sampaolo with a clear right to the title. And now I'll tell you a secret. Would you like me to tell you a secret?" she inquired.

"I can tell *you* a secret that will soon be a matter of public notoriety," said the Commendatore. "And that is that you 've clean gone out of your senses."

"The lady he is engaged to in England," said Susanna, "guess who she is. I give it to you in a million."

"How the devil can I guess who she is?" said the Commendatore.

"Well, then, listen," said Susanna. "You must n't faint, or explode, or anything—but the lady he's engaged to in England is your old friend—that bold adventuress, that knightess errant—the widow Torrebianca."

"*Domeniddio!*" gasped the Commendatore, falling back in his chair.

And I half think he would have pulled his moustaches out by their roots if Susanna had n't interceded with him to spare them.

"Don't—don't," she pleaded. "You won't have any left."

"*Domeniddio!*" he gasped three separate times, on three separate notes.

"If you're surprised," said Susanna, "think how much more surprised he will be."

"*Do-men-id-dio!*" said the Commendatore, in a whisper.

And then a servant came to announce that luncheon was ready.

XXIV

That morning Anthony had received a letter from Miss Sandus. It was dated and postmarked Craford, where, indeed, (although Miss Sandus was now at Isola Nobile), it had been written. It had been written at Susanna's request, almost under her dictation. Then she had given it to a confidential servant, with orders that it should be committed to the post three days after her departure.

"I sometimes forget, my dear," Miss Sandus had improved the occasion to remark, "that you are not English; but the Italian in you comes out in your unconquerable passion for intrigue."

The initial and principal paragraph of the letter ran as follows:—

"Do you remember once upon a time complaining to me of your lady-love that she was rich? and setting up her wealth as an obstacle to your happy wooing?—and how I pooh-poohed the notion? Well, now, it would appear, that obstacle is by way of being removed. You will have learned in your copy-book days that Fortune is a mighty uncertain goddess. And I am writing by Susanna's desire to let you know that circumstances have quite suddenly arisen which make it seem likely that she may be in some danger, if not actually on the point, of losing nearly everything that she possesses. I don't altogether clearly understand the matter, but it springs from some complication in her family, and a question whether a rather distant relative has n't a better claim than her own upon the properties she has been enjoying. She wishes me to tell you this, because, as she says, 'It may make some difference in his plans.' I am well aware, of course, as I have assured her, that it will make none—unless, indeed, it may intensify your impatience for an early wedding-day. But she insists upon my writing; and when she insists, I notice that no one ever for very long resists. What is that mysterious virtue, which some people have in abundance, (but most of us so abundantly lack), by which one is compelled, if they say *go*, to go, if they say *come*, to come? There is a question for you to meditate, as you walk by the shores of the Adriatic, under 'the golden leaves of the olives.' I wonder whether you will recollect from what poet that is quoted—'the golden leaves of the olives.' Well, they *are* golden in certain lights."

I dare say Anthony was still digesting his letter from Miss Sandus, when it was followed by the somewhat startling visit of Commendatore Fregi; and perhaps he was still under the impression of that, when, in the afternoon, he was summoned from a game of tennis, to receive the communication which I transcribe below, from the Contessa di Sampaolo. It was brought to him by a Capuchin friar, a soft-spoken, aged man, with a long milk-white beard, who said he would wait for an answer.

The Pontes, their tennis thus interrupted, strolled off towards the stables, leading Adrian with them,—an Adrian consumed, I fancy, by curiosity to know what business a Capuchin friar might have to transact with his friend. "Of course it is something to do with the plots and plans of my lady," he reflected; "but exactly *what*? If people take you into their confidence, they ought to take you into the entirety of it, and keep you *au courant* as the theme develops."

Anthony paused for an instant to admire his correspondent's strong, clear-flowing, determined hand; and then, in that stiff-jointed, formal Tuscan of the schools, which no human being was ever heard to speak, but educated Italians will persist in writing, he read:—

"Illustrissimo Signore e caro Cugino"—Nay, better translate:—

"Most Illustrious Sir and dear Cousin: From my earliest childhood I have always felt that the Revolution of 1850 was accompanied by great injustices, and particularly that, without reference to the political changes, there should have been no transfer of the hereditaments of our family from the legal heir, your Excellency's father, then a minor, to his uncle, my grandfather. At the age of twelve I made a vow, before the shrine of our Sainted Progenitor, that if ever the power to do so should be mine, I would set this injustice right.

"By the testament of my father, however, I was left under the control of a guardian until I was twenty-two, which age I attained in April last. Since April I have been constantly in the intention of restoring to the head of my family the properties that are rightly his. But many impeding circumstances, besides the dissuasions of friends whose age and wisdom I was concerned to regard, have detained me until now, when, learning that your Excellency is sojourning in the island, I feel that I must no longer postpone an act of due reparation.

"As I am but the life-tenant of these estates, and as your Excellency, being my nearest male kinsman, is legally my heir-apparent, (though morally always the head of our house), I can, I am informed, make the estates over to you by entering a Religious Order, and taking vows of celibacy for life. The small fortune which I have inherited from my mother will provide me with the dowry necessary to this step.

"Most Illustrious Sir and dear Cousin, it would give me great pleasure to make the acquaintance of your Excellency, and to do homage to the Chief of the House of San Guido, before my retirement from the world. The good Father Angelo, who bears this letter, who has my full confidence and approves of my purpose, will bring me your Excellency's answer, to say if and when you will honour me with your presence at Isola Nobile.

"I beg leave to subscribe myself. Most Illustrious Sir and dear Cousin, with sentiments of distinguished respect and affection, of your Lordship's Excellency the good cousin,

"S. del Valdeschi della Spina,
Contessa di Sampaolo."

"Al Illmo. Signore, S. E. il Conte di Sampaolo,
Alla Villa del Ponte, Vallanza."

Anthony, his cousin's letter held at arm's length, turned to the white-bearded Capuchin, where he stood in his brown habit, patiently waiting, with his clasped hands covered by his sleeves.

"My dear Father," he said, speaking quickly, his face white, his eyes troubled, "the Countess tells me that you have her full confidence and approve her purpose. But do you *know* what purpose she has intimated here?"

"Yes," said Father Angelo, calmly, bowing his head.

"But then," Anthony hurried on, his excitement unconcealed, "it is impossible you should approve it—it is impossible any one should approve it. She must be stopped. The thing she proposes to do is out of all reason. I cannot allow it. Her friends must not allow it. Her friends must prevent it."

"The thing she proposes to do is an act of simple justice," said the Father, in his soft voice.

Anthony waved his arms, intolerantly.

"Simple justice—or simple madness," he said, "it is a thing that must not even be discussed. She is twenty-two years old—she is a child—she is irresponsible—she does n't, she can't, know what she is doing. She proposes to impoverish herself, to condemn herself to a convent for life, and, so far as one can see, without the slightest vocation. Her friends must restrain her."

"She is not a person easily restrained, when she has made up her mind," said the Father, quietly.

"At all events," said Anthony, "she will be restrained in spite of herself, if the fact is impressed upon her that the sacrifice she contemplates making on my behalf is one that I will not accept—that no man could accept. She can't make her properties over to me if I refuse to accept them."

"No, I suppose she cannot," said Father Angelo. His hand came forth from his sleeve, to stroke his beard, thoughtfully. "But the properties are in all right and justice yours. Why should you not accept them? You are the legitimate Conte di Sampaolo. You are entitled to your own."

"My dear Father!" Anthony cried out, almost writhing. "It is a matter, I tell you, that I cannot even discuss. Accept them! And allow an inexperienced young girl, who can't possibly understand the consequences of her action, on a quixotic impulse, to beggar herself for me, to give up everything, to retire from the world and die by slow inches in a convent! The thing is too monstrous. A man could never hold up his head again."

"It would be well," said the Father, slowly, "if you were to tell her this in person. You had better see her, and tell her it in person."

"When can I see her?" Anthony asked, impetuous.

"When you will. She much desires to see you," the Father answered.

"The sooner, the better," said Anthony. "The sooner she definitely and permanently dismisses this folly from her mind, the better for every one concerned."

"Possibly you could go with me now?" the Father suggested. "Her launch, which brought me here, attends at the end of the garden."

"Certainly I will go with you now," said Anthony. "Wait while I put on a coat."

He ran back to the tennis-court, caught up his coat, and donned it. Then, all heated and in flannels as he was, he accompanied Father Angelo to the launch.

XXV

Susanna, Miss Sandus, a white peacock, and six ring-doves were taking refreshments in the garden, in the shade of an oleander-tree. There were cakes, figs, and lemonade, grains of dried maize, and plenty of good succulent hemp-seed. The ring-doves liked the hemp-seed and the maize, but the white peacock seemed to prefer sponge-cake soaked in lemonade.

"I know a literary man who once taught a peacock to eat sponge-cake soaked in absinthe," Miss Sandus remarked, on a key of reminiscence.

"Really? An unprincipled French literary man, I suppose?" was Susanna's natural inference.

"No, that's the funny part of it," said Miss Sandus. "He is an eminent and highly respectable English literary man, and the father of a family into the bargain. I dare n't give his name, lest he might have the law of me."

"He ought to have been ashamed of himself," Susanna said. "What became of the poor peacock? Did it descend to a drunkard's grave?"

"That's a long story," said Miss Sandus. "When you 're married and come to stay with me in Kensington, I 'll ask the literary man to dinner. Perhaps he 'll give you his account of the affair. Ah, here 's your ambassador returned," she exclaimed all at once, as Father Angelo, his beads swinging beside him, appeared advancing down the pathway.

"Well, Father——?" Susanna questioned, looking at him with eyes that were dark and anxious.

"Your cousin is a very headstrong person," said Father Angelo. "He refuses to accept your offer. He swept it aside like a whirlwind."

"Ah,—who told you he would?" crowed Miss Sandus.

"He is here to speak with you in person. He is waiting in the loggia," said Father Angelo.

Susanna leaned back in her chair. She had turned very pale.

"I think I am going to faint," she said.

"For mercy's sake, *don't*," Miss Sandus implored her, starting.

"I won't," Susanna promised, drawing a deep breath. "But you will admit I have some provocation. Must I—must I see him?"

"*Must* you?" cried Miss Sandus. "Are n't you *dying* to see him?"

"Yes," Susanna confessed, with a flutter of laughter. "I 'm dying to see him. But I 'm so *afraid*."

"I 'll disappear," said Miss Sandus, rising. "Then the good Father can bring him to you."

"Oh, don't—don't leave me," Susanna begged, stretching out her hand.

"My dear!" laughed Miss Sandus, and she tripped off towards the Palace.

"Well, Father," Susanna said, after a pause, "will you show him the way?"

The loggia, as Father Angelo called it, where he had left Anthony, while he went to announce his arrival, was the same long open colonnade in which, that morning, Susanna had had her conference with Commendatore Fregi. It was arranged as a sort of out-of-doors living-room. There were rugs on the marble pavement, and chairs and tables; and on the tables, besides vases with flowers, and other things, there were a good many books.

Absently, mechanically, (as one will when one is waiting in a strange place where books are within reach), Anthony picked a book up. It was an old, small book, in tree-calf, stamped, in the midst of much elaborate gold tooling, with the Valdeschi arms and coronet. Half-consciously examining it, he became aware presently that it was a volume of the poems of Ronsard. And then somehow it fell open, at a page that was marked by the insertion of an empty envelope.

The envelope caught Anthony's eye, and held it; and that was scarcely to be wondered at, for, in his own unmistakable handwriting, it was addressed to Madame Torrebianca, at the New Manor, Craford, England, and its upper corner bore an uncancelled twenty-five centime Italian postage-stamp.

On the page the envelope marked was printed the sonnet, "Voicy le Bois."

What happened at this moment in Anthony's head and heart? Many things must have become rather violently and painfully clear to him; many things must have changed their aspect, and adjusted themselves in new combinations. Many things that had seemed trifling or meaningless must have assumed significance and importance. No doubt he was shaken by many tumultuous thoughts and feelings. But outwardly he appeared almost unmoved. He returned the book to the table, and began to walk backwards and forwards, his head bowed a little, as one considering. Sometimes he would give a brief low laugh. Sometimes he would look up, frown, and vaguely shake his fist. Once, shaking his fist, he muttered, "Oh, that

Adrian!" And once, with a delighted chuckle, "By Jove, how awfully she 'll be dished!"

Then Father Angelo came back.

"The Countess is in the garden. May I show you the way?" he said.

But when they had reached the marble bridge that connects the garden with the Palace, "I think it will be best if you see her alone," the Father said. "Cross this bridge, and keep straight up the path beyond, and you will come to her."

"Thank you, Father," said Anthony, and crossed the bridge.

He crossed the marble bridge, and kept straight up the path beyond. And there, at the end of the path, in the shade of an oleander-tree, with her back towards him, stood a young woman—a young woman in a pearl-grey frock, and a garden-hat, beneath which one could see that her hair was dark. Young women's backs, however, in this world, to the undiscerning eyes of men, are apt to present no immediately recognizable characteristic features; and so if it had n't been for Ronsard, I don't know what would have happened.

It was very still in the garden. The birds were taking their afternoon siesta. The breeze faintly lisped in the tree-tops. Even the sunshine, as if it were not always still, seemed stiller than its wont.

"Oh, what—what—what will he think, what will he say, what will he do, when I turn round, and he sees who I am?" The question repeated and repeated itself in Susanna's mind, rhythmically, to the tremulous beating of her heart, as she heard Anthony's footsteps coming near.

He walked quickly, but a few paces short of where she stood he halted, and for a breathing-space or two there was silence.

Then at last, in English, in his smoothest, his most detached, his most languid manner, but with an overtone of exultancy that could not be subdued, he said—

"These ingenuous attempts at mystification are immensely entertaining; but are there to be many more of them, before you can permit our little comedy to reach its happy dénouement?"

"Good heavens!" thought Susanna, wildly.

She did n't turn round, but presently her shoulders began to shake. She could n't help it. The discomfiture was hers; she had been "awfully dished" indeed. But her shoulders shook and shook with silent laughter.

In the end, of course, she turned.

In her dark eyes disappointment, satisfaction, amazement, and amusement shone together.

"How in the world did you find out?" she asked. "How *could* you have found out? When did you find out? How long have you known? And if you knew, why did you pretend not to know?"

But Anthony, at the sight of her face, forgot everything.

"Oh, never mind," he cried, and advanced upon her with swift strides.

By-and-by, "Let me look at your right hand," said Susanna. "I want to see whether you have the Valdeschi pit."

"The Valdeschi what?" said Anthony.

"The Valdeschi pit," said she.

"What is that?" he asked.

"The Valdeschi pit!" she exclaimed. "Do you mean to say that you, the head of the family, don't know?"

"What is it?" he asked.

"Every true-born son or daughter of San Guido," she explained, "bears in the palm of the hand a little pit or dint, which is the survival in his descendants of the scar made by the thorn in the hand of San Guido himself. See—I have it."

She held out her hand.

Anthony took it, bent ever it, kissed it, studied it.

"It is a delicious hand—but I see no pit," he said.

"*There*," said she, placing the tip of her finger upon a tiny concavity in the rose-white flesh.

"That?" laughed Anthony. "That is nothing but a pretty little dimple."

"Oh, no," said she, seriously. "That is the mark of the Valdeschi. I 'm sure you have it too—we all have it. Let me see."

She took his lean brown hand, and examined it carefully, eagerly.

"There! I was sure!" she cried.

She pointed to where, in a position corresponding to that of the "mark of the Valdeschi" in her own hand, there was an indentation that looked like a half-obliterated scar.

Presently, in the direction of the Palace, a bell began to ring, rather a deep-toned bell, like a church-bell.

Susanna rose.

"When you were here the other day as a mere visitor," she said, "I suppose they did n't show you the chapel, did they?"

"No," said Anthony.

"They don't show it to mere visitors," she went on. "But come with me now, and you shall see it. Father Angelo is going to give Benediction. That is what the bell is ringing for."

She led the way towards the Palace. As they were crossing the bridge, "Look," she said, and pointed to a flagstaff that sprang from the highest pinnacle of the building. A flag was being hoisted there; and now it fluttered forth and flew in the breeze, a red flag with a design in gold upon it.

"The flag of the Count of Sampaolo: gules, a spine or," said Susanna. "Of course you know why they are flying it now?"

"No—?" wondered Anthony.

"Because the Count of Sampaolo is at home," she said.

Then they went in to Benediction.

9 789356 575486